A SURPRISE FOR THE SHEIKH

SARAH M. ANDERSON

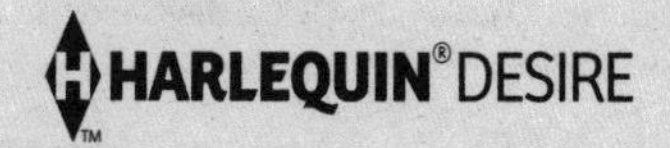

Special thanks and acknowledgment are given to
Sarah M. Anderson for her contribution to the
Texas Cattleman's Club: Lies and Lullabies series.

ISBN-13: 978-0-373-73452-8

A Surprise for the Sheikh

This edition published by arrangement with Harlequin Books S.A.

For questions and comments about the quality of this book, please contact us at CustomerService@Harlequin.com.

Printed in U.S.A.

Sarah M. Anderson may live east of the Mississippi River, but her heart lies out West on the Great Plains. Sarah's book *A Man of Privilege* won an RT Reviewers' Choice Best Book Award in 2012.

Sarah spends her days having conversations with imaginary cowboys and American Indians. Find out more about Sarah's love of cowboys and Indians at sarahmanderson.com and sign up for the new-release newsletter at eepurl.com/nv39b.

Books by Sarah M. Anderson

HARLEQUIN DESIRE

The Nanny Plan
His Forever Family

Texas Cattleman's Club: Lies and Lullabies

A Surprise for the Sheikh

The Bolton Brothers

Straddling the Line
Bringing Home the Bachelor
Expecting a Bolton Baby

The Beaumont Heirs

Not the Boss's Baby
Tempted by a Cowboy
A Beaumont Christmas
His Son, Her Secret
Falling for Her Fake Fiancé

Visit her Author Profile page at Harlequin.com, or sarahmanderson.com, for more titles!

To Dad, who taught me the importance of never saying “very” when “damn” would do.

Prologue

This was really happening.

Ben's hot body pressed Violet against the back of the elevator. Something hard and long bumped against her hip, and she giggled. Oh, yeah—this was *so* happening.

She was really doing this.

"Kiss me," Ben said in that sinfully delicious accent of his as he flexed his hips against hers. She didn't know where he was from, but his accent made her think of the burning heat of summer sun—because boy, did it warm her up.

Violet ran her hands through his thick black hair and lifted his face away from where he'd been sucking on her neck.

He touched his forehead to hers. "Kiss me, my mysterious, my beautiful V." Then—incredibly—he hesitated just long enough to make it clear he was waiting for her decision.

Power surged through her. This was exactly why she was riding in an elevator in the Holloway Inn up to a man's room—a man who did not know she was Violet McCallum, who did not know she was Mac McCallum's baby sister.

Her entire life, she had been Violet. Violet, who had to be protected from the big bad world. Violet, the lost little girl whose parents died and left her all alone. Violet, who still lived at home and still had her big brother watching over her every move to make sure she didn't get hurt again.

Well, to hell with that. Tonight, she was V. She was mysterious, she was beautiful, and this man—this sinfully handsome man with an accent like liquid sunshine—wanted her to kiss him.

She was not Violet. Not tonight.

So she kissed him, long and hard, their tongues tangling in her mouth, then in his. She did more than kiss him—she raked her fingers through his hair and held him against her. She made it clear—this was what she wanted. He was what she wanted.

She hadn't come to this hotel bar a town away from Royal, Texas, with the intent of going to bed with a stranger. She hadn't planned on a one-night stand. She'd wanted to get dressed up, to feel pretty—maybe to flirt. She'd wanted to be someone else, just for the night.

But she hadn't counted on Ben. "You have beautiful eyes," he said in his sunshine voice, his hands sliding down her backside and cupping her bottom. "Among other things, my mysterious V." Then he lifted, and it was only natural that her legs went around his waist and that the long, hard bulge in his pants went from bumping against her thigh to pressing against the spot at her very center.

Violet's back arched as heat radiated throughout her body. Ben held tight to her, pinning her back against the elevator wall as he pressed his mouth to the cleavage that this little black dress left exposed. One of the hands that was cupping her bottom slid forward, snagging on the hem of her dress as he stroked between her legs. The heat from his hand only added to the raging inferno taking place under her skin.

"If you leave this elevator, you will be mine, you understand? I will lay you out on the bed and make you cry out. This is your last chance to take the elevator down."

A shiver of delight raced through her. Respectable Violet would never let a man talk to her like this. But V? "Is that a promise?"

"It is," he said in such a serious tone that she gasped. "Your pleasure is my pleasure."

That was, hands down, the sweetest thing anyone had ever whispered to her. Her entire life had been one long exercise in telling people what she wanted only to have to listen to the litany of excuses why she couldn't do what she wanted or couldn't have what she wanted. It was too risky, too dangerous. She didn't understand the consequences, she didn't this, she didn't that—every excuse her brother could throw at her, he did.

If Mac knew she was in this elevator with a man whose pleasure was her pleasure—well, there might be guns involved. This was risky and dangerous and all that stuff that Mac had spent the past twelve years trying to shield her from.

She was tired of being protected. She wanted something more than safety.

She wanted Ben.

"Why are we still in this elevator?" she asked in as

innocent a tone as she could muster, given how Ben's body was pressing against hers.

"You are quite certain?"

"Quite. But don't stop talking." The words hadn't even gotten out of her mouth before Ben hauled her away from the wall of the elevator and out into the hall.

"Are you this adventurous in everything?"

He was carrying her as if she weighed nothing at all. She was as light as a feather, a leaf on the wind, in Ben's arms. She was flying and she didn't ever want to come down.

She also didn't want to cop to her relatively limited experiences in the whole "pleasure" department. Every time she got serious about a guy, her brother—her well-meaning, overbearing brother—came down like the hammer of Thor and before Violet could blink, the guy would be giving her the it's-not-you-it's-me talk.

Violet may have had only a couple of boyfriends, but V was knowledgeable and experienced. She could not only handle a man like Ben, she could meet him as an equal. And so help her, no one was going to give her the let's-be-friends talk tonight. "Why don't we find out?"

He growled against her neck.

A door opened. "What's—" an older man, voice heavy on the Texas accent, said.

Ben stopped and, without putting Violet down, turned to stare at the old man in the open doorway. He didn't say anything. He didn't make a menacing gesture. He just stared down the other man.

"Ah. Well. Yes," the older man babbled as the door shut.

"Whoa," Violet said, giggling again. "Dude, you are—wow." So this was what exuding masculinity looked like.

"'Dude,' eh?" Ben said with a sexy chuckle as he

began walking down the hall. Every step made Violet gasp as Ben's hard length pressed against her sex. "For a woman as beautiful as you, you often talk like a man."

"I don't always wear little black dresses."

Ben stopped in front of another door. "Hmm," he said as his hands stayed on her body as he set her down, which effectively meant he hiked her dress up. "Are you sure you won't tell me your name?"

"No," she said quickly. She didn't want this fantasy night of perfection to be ruined by something as mundane as reality. "No names. Not tonight."

He got his key out and opened the door. Then his hands were back on her body, walking her backward into the room. "Who are you hiding from? Family?" He pulled her to a stop and turned her around. His fingers found her zipper and pulled it down, one slow click after another. "Or another lover, hmm?"

"I'm not hiding from anyone," she fibbed. It was a small fib because, no, she did not want Mac to know she'd done something this wild, this crazy. That's why she was in Holloway instead of Royal.

"We are all hiding from something, are we not?" Ben began to pull the dress down, revealing the black bra with the white embroidery that she wore only when she was feeling particularly rebellious. Which, in the last few months, was almost every day.

"I just—look," she said in frustration, taking a step back and pulling free of his hands. "I won't ask about you, you won't ask about me, and we use condoms. That's the deal. If that doesn't work for you…" She grabbed the sleeves of her dress and tugged them back up.

Ben stood there, his sinfully delicious lips curved into a smile. Oh, no—he wouldn't call her bluff, would he?

Because she wanted to strip him out of that suit—and she didn't want to walk out of this room until she was barely able to walk at all.

"I just need a night with you," she said, the truth of that statement sinking in for the first time since she'd walked into the bar at the Holloway Inn and laid eyes on this tall, dark and handsome stranger. She'd thought she just needed a night out, but the very moment Ben had turned to her, his coal-black eyes taking in her lacy black cocktail dress, her wavy auburn hair, her stockings with the seam up the back—then she'd needed him. And she wasn't going to rest until she had him. "That's all I'm asking. One night. No strings. Just…pleasure."

Ben stepped into her, cupping her face in his hands. "That is really all you want from me? Nothing else?"

The way he said it, with a touch of sadness in his voice, made her heart ache for him. She didn't know who he was or why he was here—he wasn't local, that much was obvious. But she got the feeling that in his real life, there were always strings.

She knew the feeling. And for tonight, at least, she didn't want to be hemmed in by other people's expectations of her. Good idea or not, she was going to take Ben to bed. There would be no regrets. Not for her. "No. Your pleasure is my pleasure," she whispered against his lips, turning his words back to him.

"Kiss me," he said against her skin.

So she did. She tangled her hands in his hair and pulled him roughly against her mouth, and then they were flinging each other's clothing off and falling into bed and she couldn't tell where her pleasure began and his ended because Ben was everything she'd ever dreamed a lover could be, only better—hotter, sweeter.

She fell asleep in his arms, listening to him whisper

stories to her in a language she did not know and did not understand, but it didn't matter. She was sated and happy. She'd started this night desperate to do something fun, something for herself.

Ben—no last name, no country of origin—was an answer to her prayers.

One

Four months later

This was *not* happening.

Dear God, please let this not be happening. Violet stared down at the thin strip of plastic. The one that said in digital block letters, *PREGNANT.*

Maybe she'd done it wrong. Peed on the wrong end or something. Yeah, that was it. She'd never taken a pregnancy test before. She hadn't even studied. She'd failed due to a lack of preparation, that was all.

Luckily, Violet had bought three separate tests because redundancy wasn't just redundant. It was confirmation that her night of wild passion four months ago with a stranger named Ben had not left her pregnant.

Crouched in the bathroom off of her bedroom, Violet carefully read the instructions again, trying to spot her mistake. Remove the purple cap: check. Hold the other end: check. Hold absorbent tip downward: check. Wait two minutes: check.

Crap. She'd done it right.

So she did it again.

The next two minutes were hell. The panic was so strong she could practically taste it in the back of her throat, and it was getting stronger with every passing second.

The first test was just a false positive, she decided. False positives happened all the time. She wasn't pregnant. She was suffering from a low-grade stomach bug. Yeah, that was it. That would explain the odd waves of nausea that hit her at unexpected times. Not in the morning either. Therefore, it wasn't morning sickness.

And the low-grade bug she was fighting—that's what caused the positive. It had absolutely nothing to do with that night in the Holloway Inn four months ago. It had nothing to do with Ben or V or…

PREGNANT.

Oh, God.

One was a false positive. The second? Considering that she'd had a wild night of passionate sex with a man in a hotel room?

What the hell was she going to do?

She didn't have a last name. She didn't have his number. He'd been this fantasy man who had appeared when she'd needed him and been gone by morning light. She'd woken up in his room alone. Her dress had been cleaned and pressed and was hanging on the bathroom door. Room service had delivered breakfast with a rose and a note—a note she still had, tucked inside her sock drawer, where Mac would never see it.

Your pleasure was my pleasure. Thank you for the night.

He hadn't even signed it Ben. No name, no signature. No way to contact him when she had a rapidly growing collection of positive pregnancy tests on the edge of her sink.

She was screwed.

Okay, so contacting Ben was out, at least for the short term. She might be able to hire a private investigator who could track him down through the hotel's guest registry, but that didn't help her out right now.

"Violet?" Mac called out from downstairs. "Can you come down here?"

She was going to be sick again, and this time she didn't think it was because of morning sickness.

How was she supposed to tell her big brother that she'd done something this wild and crazy and was now pregnant? The man had dedicated the past twelve years of his life to keeping her safe after their parents' deaths. He would not react well.

"Violet?" She heard the creak of the second step—oh Lord, he was on his way up.

"Give me a minute!" she called through the door as she grabbed the two used tests and shoved them back in the box. She hid everything under the sink, behind her maxi pads. Mac would never look there.

She needed a plan. She was on her own here.

Violet stood up and quickly splashed some cold water on her face. She didn't normally wear a lot of makeup. She had no need to look pretty when she was managing the Double M, their family ranch. The ranch hands she'd hired had all gotten the exact same message, no doubt—hitting on Mac McCallum's little sister was strictly forbidden. Which irritated her. First off, she wasn't hiring studs for the express purpose of getting it on in the hayloft. Second, she was the boss. Mac ran McCallum Enterprises, the energy company their father had founded, and Violet ran the Double M, and the less those two worlds crossed, the better it was.

Because Mac did not see a ranch manager, much less a damned good ranch manager. He didn't see a capable businesswoman who was navigating a drought and rebuilding from a record-breaking tornado and still making a profit. He didn't see a partner in the family business.

All he saw was the shattered sixteen-year-old girl she'd been when their parents had died. It didn't matter what she did, how well she did it—she was still a little sister to him. Nothing more and nothing less.

Violet had wanted so desperately not to be Mac's helpless baby sister, even for a night. And if that night was spent in a stranger's arms…

And here she was.

She'd just jerked her ponytail out of its holder and started wrenching the brush through her mane of auburn hair when Mac said, "Violet?"

She jumped. She hadn't heard Mac come the rest of the way upstairs, but now he was right outside the door. "What?"

"An old friend of mine is downstairs. Rafe."

"Oh—okay," she said, feeling confused. Rafe—why did that name sound familiar? And why did Mac sound… odd? "Is everything okay?"

Ha. Nothing was okay, but by God, until she got a grip on the situation, she was going to pretend it was if it was the last thing she did.

"No, it's fine. It's just—Rafe is the sheikh, you remember? From college?"

"Wait." She cracked the door open and stared at her brother. Even though she'd hidden the evidence, she intentionally positioned her body between him and the sink. "Is this the guy who had the wild younger sister who tricked you? *That* Rafe?"

"Yeah. Rafiq bin Saleed." Mac's expression was a mix of excitement and confusion.

"What's he doing here right now?" Violet asked. "I mean, correct me if I'm wrong, but didn't he blame you for his sister's—what did you call it?"

"Compromising her innocence? Yeah."

"So why do I have to meet this jerk?"

"He's in town. He's apologized for his behavior years ago."

Violet stared at him. Men and their delicate attempts at friendship. "And you're okay with that?"

"Yeah," Mac said with a shrug. "Why wouldn't I be? It was a misunderstanding. His father was the one who was mad. Rafe is making amends."

After twelve years? That seemed odd. *Men.* "And you're warning me in advance because..."

"Because I know you, Violet. I know you're liable to shoot your mouth off. He's a sheikh—they have a different set of customs, okay? So try to be polite."

She gave him a dull look. "Really? You think I'm so impulsive I can't even make small talk with a man from a different culture?" She shoved the door open. Her hair could wait. "Thanks, Mac. I appreciate the vote of confidence there."

Mac grinned at her. "Said Violet, impulsively."

"Stuff it. Let's get this over with." She pushed past her brother and stomped to the closet, where she grabbed a clean shirt. If she was going to be meeting—wait, what was a sheikh? Were they royalty? Well, whatever he was, the least she could do was make sure she was wearing a shirt that didn't have cow poop on it. "I'll meet your rude sheikh friend and then make myself scarce, okay? I've got stuff to do anyway." Like maybe tracking down her one-night stand and figuring out her due date and, well, her schedule was just *packed.* She started unbuttoning her work jeans.

The wheels of her mind spun. This was going to change everything. She'd had plans—she'd been slowly working on convincing her brother to buy the ranch to the north, the Wild Aces. Violet had loved the Wild Aces for years. She wanted out of this house, out from under Mac's overprotective roof, and the Wild Aces was where she wanted to be.

They were already leasing the land. The Double M's water supply had been compromised by the tornado last year. But Wild Aces had plenty of water. Violet had thought that would be the motivation Mac needed to sign off on the purchase, but because she was the one who'd suggested it instead of his assistant, Andrea Beaumont, Mac had said no. Eventually, the two women had convinced Mac to at least lease the land.

But now? Violet was pregnant. How was she going to manage the Double M, much less the Wild Aces, with a huge belly or a baby on her hip?

Mac didn't say anything for so long she paused and looked up at him. "What?"

"Everything okay?" he asked.

She tensed. "Why wouldn't it be? It's fine. Totally fine."

Mac wrinkled his brow at her but before he could question her further, she said, "Shouldn't you be downstairs with your sheikh friend or something? So I can finish getting changed? Maybe?"

Mac paled. He may have stepped into the role of father figure after their parents' deaths, but he was still a big brother. An irritating one at that.

Okay, so she had a plan. She was going to pretend everything was just hunky-dory for the foreseeable future while she thought of a better plan.

Where was Ben? And even if she could find him, would he be happy to see her? Or would he claim that their night had had no strings attached and a baby was a huge string and therefore, she was on her own?

What a freaking mess.

"Sorry about that," Mac said, strolling back into the room. "Violet's…well, she's Violet."

Rafe sat in the center of the couch, surveying the room and the man before him. Mac had most certainly aged in the past twelve years, but he didn't have the haunted look of someone who had betrayed his best friend.

Rafe was not surprised, not really. At the time Mac compromised Nasira, he had exhibited little regard for Rafe's family's name. He did not look guilty because, more than likely, Mac McCallum was incapable of feeling guilt.

Revenge was a dish best served cold. But Rafe couldn't overplay his hand here. He put on a warm smile and said, "Yes, your younger sister—I remember. She was still in high school when we were at college, correct?"

"Yeah, that's right." Mac shrugged apologetically. If Rafe were capable of being sympathetic with a person such as Mac, he could sympathize over wayward younger sisters. "So," Mac went on, changing the subject. "Tell me about you, man. It's been years! What are you doing in town?"

Rafe shrugged, as if his being in Royal, Texas, were

some sort of happy accident instead of entirely premeditated. "My father is dead," he said.

Mac's cheeks reddened. "Oh, dude—sorry about that."

Rafe smiled—inwardly, of course. The last person to say "dude" to him in such a way had been V, the beautiful woman at the inn a few months ago. It had seemed so odd coming out of her perfect rosebud mouth. It was much better suited to a man like Mac.

Where was V now? That was a question that had danced at the edge of his consciousness for months. He had gotten better at putting the question aside, though. It was almost easy to not think of her. Almost.

"I appreciate your concern, but there is no need for sorrow. He was a...difficult man, as I'm sure you know."

Mac nodded sympathetically. In fact, before Mac's betrayal of Rafe's family, Mac had been one of the few people Rafe had confided in about his "difficult" father. There had been a time, long ago, when Rafe would have trusted this man with his very life.

Rafe did not trust people. He had learned that lesson well. Years spent locked up by his father had taught him that.

"With his passing," Rafe went on, "my older brother Fareed became the sheikh and I became more free to seek my way in the world." He tried to make it sound carefree and, in truth, some of it had been. Fareed had turned his attention to the modernization of their sheikhdom and released Rafe. Fareed had even entrusted Rafe with control of the family shipping business. All things considered, the reversal of fortune had been breathtaking.

But just because Rafe had no longer had to deal with Hassad bin Saleed did not mean he was free. He was still a sheikh. He had his people's honor and pride to preserve.

And if that meant waiting twelve years to exact his revenge, then so be it.

"I had meant to seek you out much earlier," Rafe went on, bending the truth until it was on the verge of breaking. "But my brother gave me the shipping company and I was quite busy turning the business around. You understand how it is. I am expanding my company's holdings and was looking to get into energy. The worldwide demand is rising. Naturally, I thought of you. I remember how fondly you spoke of this area and its many resources."

That was his story. Secretly, Rafe had been buying up land all over Royal, Texas, under the front of Samson Oil, a company he had created ostensibly to purchase the mineral rights and whatever remaining oil existed underground.

But Samson Oil was buying lands that had no more oil and no valuable mineral rights to speak of. The land was good for little else besides grazing cattle, and the entire town knew it. He had hired a Royal native, Nolan Dane, to act as the public face of Samson Oil. The townsfolk had been easily swayed by the outrageous offers and Nolan's down-home charm. They were happy to take his money—except, of course, that no one knew it was *his* money. By the time they figured out his scheme, it would be too late.

Rafe would own this town, and he would do with it as he saw fit.

Mac snorted. "Tell me about it. McCallum Enterprises has completely taken over my life. I can't even run the ranch anymore—Violet handles that for me."

"Your younger sister does a man's job?" But he was not truly surprised. Mac had always spoken of how outlandish his baby sister was—a tomboy, he'd said.

"She does a damn good job, too," Mac said in a thoughtful voice.

"I had thought she was going to follow you to Harvard." That had been the story Mac had told him all those years ago. But had that just been a lie to earn Rafe's trust as they bonded over difficult younger siblings?

"That was before our parents died. They went out for a flight on Dad's plane and..." Mac sighed heavily. "She was so lost after the accident, you know? I hated that I wasn't here for her when it happened."

"I had not realized," Rafe said sympathetically, even though of course he had realized. The McCallum family had suffered a terrible blow when Mac's parents' plane had crashed into an open field. There had been no survivors.

It all happened right after Rafe had been pulled out of Harvard by his father for daring to let his younger sister consort with the likes of Mac. Rafe had not found out the details of the accident for years afterward—after his own father had died and Rafe had suddenly had the means to investigate his enemies.

It had been a missed opportunity. If Rafe had been aware of the McCallums' deaths at the time, he could have moved swiftly to buy Mac's land out from under him or take over McCallum Enterprises. Instead, Rafe had to settle for watching and waiting for his next best opportunity to exact his revenge. He had not rushed. He was, as the Americans often said, playing the long game.

His patience had finally paid off when, last year, a tornado had torn through Mac's hometown of Royal, Texas. The town's economic base was weakened, which was good. But what was better was that Mac's water supply had become compromised.

It was a particularly good scheme. Rafe would not only cut off Mac's water supply and essentially strangle his ranch, but under the guise of Samson Oil, he would also buy up large parts of Royal. Mac had always spoken of his love for his hometown.

When Rafe was done with him, Mac would have nothing. No town, no land. That was what Mac had left Nasira with when he had betrayed Rafe's trust and ruined Nasira.

Thus far, Rafe had been operating in secrecy. But when his scheme came to fruition, he wanted Mac to know it was he who had brought about his destruction.

Which was why he was here, pretending to be concerned for the well-being of his former friend's sister. "Was it very hard on her?"

"Oh, man," Mac said with a rueful smile. "I moved back home and tried to give her a stable upbringing, but never underestimate the power of a teenage girl. Hey, listen," he went on, leaning forward and dropping his voice a notch. "I know that things didn't end well between us..."

Rafe tensed inside but outside, he waved this poor excuse for an olive branch of peace away, as if he'd truly left the matter in the past. "It was all a long time ago. Think nothing of it."

"Thanks, man. I never meant to hurt Nasira, but I swear to you, I had no idea she was in my room that night. It wasn't what it looked like."

Rafe's mask of genial friendship must have slipped because Mac's words trailed off. Rafe rearranged his face into one of concern. "It's fine. She was able to marry a man who was more to her liking." It was time for a subject change. "Your sister, Violet? It has been a long time."

"Yeah—that's what I wanted to talk to you about. I

try to keep her out of trouble, but if you, you know, could just keep an eye on her while you're in town, I'd really appreciate it."

Now this was ironic. Here Rafe was, doing everything within his power to avenge the honor of his sister and his family, and Mac, the source of all his troubles, was asking Rafe to look after Violet?

That would be a new layer to Rafe's revenge—corrupting Mac's sister just as Mac had corrupted Rafe's.

"But of course," Rafe said as he bowed his head, trying to look touched that Mac would extend him this much trust. The fool. He was making this too easy.

"My ears are burning." Rafe heard the soft feminine—and familiar—voice seconds before its owner entered the room. "What are you two…talking…"

She stood in the doorway, her mouth open, all the color draining from her cheeks.

Rafe's body responded before his brain could make sense of what he was seeing. His gut tightened and his erection stiffened and one word presented itself in his mind—*mine*. The reaction was so sudden and so complete that Rafe was momentarily disoriented. This woman was lovely, yes, but her body was not the kind that usually invoked such an immediate, possessive response from him.

Then the conscious part of his brain caught up with the rest of him and he realized exactly who she was.

She looked different in the light of day. Rafe had not known her in such mannish clothing—jeans and work shirts. Her hair was pulled into a low ponytail at the nape of her neck and her face was scrubbed clean.

But he recognized her nonetheless.

V.

His mind spun in bewilderment. His mysterious, beautiful V was *here*? The woman he had been unable to put from his mind was…in Mac's home?

Mac stood and Rafe stood with him. This was an… unexpected development. He would have to brazen it out as best he could. "Ah, here you are. Violet, this is my old college friend, Rafe bin Saleed."

"*Bin* Saleed?" she said, her eyes so wide they were practically bursting out of her head. *"Bin?"*

"Um, yeah," Mac said, his gaze darting between the two of them. "Rafe, this is my little sister, Violet."

V was Violet. V was his mortal enemy's younger sister.

Destiny had a twisted sense of humor.

Inwardly, he was kicking himself, as the Americans said. Rafiq bin Saleed did not randomly bring a woman back to his bed. He did not seduce her and strip her and he most certainly did not send her love notes the next morning. He was a sheikh. He had no need for those things. His one night of passion with the exact wrong woman could threaten twelve years of planning.

Outwardly, however, he kept his composure. Years of facing his father's wrath had trained him well in remaining calm in the face of danger. He had to put a good face on this. His scheme had not yet come to fruition, and if Violet placed him in the greater Royal area four months before his "arrival" today, everything could be at risk.

All his schemes could fall apart in front of him, all because he had been unable to resist a beautiful woman.

Unless…a new thought occurred to him. Unless Violet already knew of his schemes. Unless she had been sent by her brother to find him all those months ago. Unless Mac had anticipated Rafe's attack and launched a counterattack while Rafe was distracted by a beautiful smile and a gorgeous body.

But she had insisted on no names. He had never used his real name, just as she had hidden hers. Was it possible that she had really just been looking for a night's passion?

He had no choice but to continue to play the part of the long-lost friend. He couldn't show his hand just because he had accidentally slept with this woman. "Violet," he said, letting the hard *T* sound of her name roll off his tongue, just as so many other things had rolled off his tongue. He bowed low to her, a sign of respect in his culture. "It is an honor to finally meet Mac's beloved sister."

"Is it?" she snapped.

Mac shot her a warning look. "Violet," he said quietly. "We talked about this."

"Sorry," she said, clearly not sorry at all. "I was expecting someone else entirely."

Rafe wanted to laugh. Truthfully, he had been, as well. But he did no such thing. Instead, he said calmly, "Have I come at a bad time?"

Americans had an expression that Rafe had never heard before he'd attended university at Harvard— "If looks could kill." In his sheikhdom of Al Qunfudhah, no one would dare look at a sheikh with such venom—to do so was to risk dismemberment or even death at the hands of Hassad bin Saleed, who had ruled with an iron fist and an iron blade.

But he was no longer in Al Qunfudhah, and if looks could kill, Violet would have finished him off several minutes ago.

He notched an eyebrow at her. He was more than capable of controlling himself. Could she say the same? Or was that why Mac had gone to speak to her privately—were they getting their stories straight?

You were *capable of controlling yourself*, a small voice in the back of his mind whispered. *Until you met her.*

"No, no," Mac said warmly. "Violet, maybe you should get us something to drink."

She turned her wrathful gaze to Mac and Rafe decided that, even if Mac had sent Violet to him, she had not told her brother the truth of their evening together. "Excuse me? Do I look like your maid?"

"Violet!" Mac sent another worried grin toward Rafe. "Sorry, Rafe."

Rafe waved his hand as if Violet's attitude were nothing. "We are not in Al Qunfudhah," he said, trying to set Mac at ease even as he enjoyed his old friend's discomfort. "I remember how things in America are quite different than they are back home. I do not expect to be served by the women in the house."

But even as he said it, he casually sat back in the middle of the sofa, spreading his arms out along the back and waiting to be served by someone. He took up as much space as he could. *I am here*, he thought at Violet, catching her eye and lifting his chin in challenge. *What are you going to do about it?*

Oh, yes. If looks could kill, he would be in extreme pain right now. "That's where you're from?"

The bitterness of her tone was somewhat unexpected. The last time he had seen her, she had been asleep in his bed, nude except for the sheets that had twisted around her waist. Her beautiful auburn hair had been fanned out over her shoulder, and even as she slept, her rosebud lips had been curved into a satisfied, if small, smile. She had looked like a woman who had been thoroughly pleasured, and Rafe had almost woken her up with a touch and a kiss.

But she had only asked for a night, so he quietly let himself out of the room, arranged to have breakfast sent up and then met with Nolan to go over his plans for purchasing more of the land around Mac's Double M ranch. He had tried mightily to put his night of wanton abandon with the beautiful V out of his mind.

Which was not to say he had succeeded. Not for the first time, he replayed their evening together. He had not coerced her—no, he specifically remembered several points where he had given her a respectable out.

It had been her choice to come to his room. Her choice to make it one night. Her choice not to use names or places.

As far as Rafe was concerned, Violet had nothing to be bitter about. He had made sure she had been well satisfied, just as he had been.

"I'll get us something to drink. Violet, can I talk to you in the kitchen?" Mac said, forgoing subtlety altogether.

"I'll take some lemonade," Violet responded, ignoring her brother's request and sitting in a chair across from Rafe. "Thanks."

Of course Rafe knew they were not in Al Qunfudhah anymore, but it was something of a surprise to not only see a woman give a man—her guardian, no less—an order, but to see that man heave a weary sigh and obey.

Perhaps if Nasira had felt freer to assert herself as Violet did…

Well, things might have been different. But knowing his father, things would not have been better.

Rafe pushed away those thoughts and focused instead on the woman before him. Violet was seething with barely contained rage, that much was obvious.

Once Mac was out of the room, Violet leaned toward him. "Rafiq *bin* Saleed?"

He would not let her get to him. She may be a slightly hysterical female, but he was still a sheikh. "It's lovely to see you again, V. Unexpected, yes, but lovely nonetheless."

"Oh, it's unexpected all right. What the hell?"

He ignored her outburst. "You are well, I trust?"

Her eyes got wide—very wide indeed. "*Well?* Oh, you're going to care now?"

He bristled at her tone. "For your information, I cared that night. But it was you who asked for just that—a night. Just one. So I honored your wishes. No names, no strings—that was how you put it, was it not?"

She continued to glare at him. "What do I even call you? Not Ben, I assume."

"Rafe will do for now."

"Will it? Is that your real name? Or just another alias?"

"My name is Rafiq," he said stiffly. He did not enjoy being on the defensive. "Rafe is a well-known nickname in my country."

Her nostrils flared, as if she were getting ready to physically attack him. "Well, Rafe, since you asked, I am not well."

"No?" Against his will, he felt a plume of concern rise through his belly. He should be glad she was not well. That would only cause Mac more suffering.

But Rafe was concerned. He wanted to pull her into his arms and feel her breath against his skin and make her well. He was a wealthy man. There was nothing he could not provide for her. "Not because of something I have done, I hope."

She was breathing hard now, as if she were standing on the top of a tall peak and getting ready to jump. "You could say that. I'm pregnant."

Rafe blinked at her, trying to comprehend the words. Had she just said—*pregnant*? "Mine?"

She looked much like a lioness ready to pounce on her

prey, all coiled energy and focus. "Of course it's yours. I realize we don't know very much about each other but I don't normally pick up men. That was a one time thing. You're the only man I've been with in the last year and *you* were supposed to use *condoms*!" She hissed the word but quietly. It was for his ears and his ears alone.

Before he could come up with something reasonable to say—something reasonable to think, even—Mac strode back into the room, carrying a tray with a pitcher and glasses. "Lemonade?"

Two

Rafe just…sat there. For Pete's sake, he didn't even blink when Mac walked back into the room. Violet's whole world was falling apart around her and Rafe looked as though she'd announced she liked French fries instead of the fact that she was carrying his child.

She couldn't take it. She needed to go. If she could make it back to a bathroom, where she could throw up in peace and quiet, that'd be great.

"Actually," she said, forcing herself to stand. "I'm not thirsty. Thanks anyway, Mac."

The father of her unborn baby was not just some nameless stranger she'd met in a bar. Oh, no—that would be getting off easy. If that were the case, she'd merely be pregnant and alone. Which was a terrifying prospect, but comparatively?

The father of her child was a sheikh. And not just any sheikh. Her brother's former friend, the one who had blamed Mac for seducing his sister and ended the friendship under no uncertain terms.

Oh, she was going to be so sick.

She willed her legs not to wobble as she stood. Ben or Rafe or Sheikh Saleed or whatever his name was stood with her.

In the past thirty-some-odd minutes, her perfect fantasy night had somehow become an epic nightmare. Had she been dreading telling Mac she was pregnant before? Ha. How the hell was she supposed to tell him now? *I'm expecting and by the way, the father is your old friend. Isn't that a laugh riot?*

Mac already treated her as though she was still a lost little girl of sixteen. What would he do now that she'd proven how very irresponsible she was?

Oh, God—this was going to change everything. It already had.

She turned and headed for the door, but due to her wobbly legs, she didn't get out of the room fast enough. "Violet," Rafe said in his ridiculous voice, all sunshine and honey, and damned if the sound of her name on his lips didn't send another burst of warmth and desire through her. Her head may have been a mess, but her body—her stupid, traitorous body—still wanted this man. Hell.

It didn't matter. She couldn't let his accent melt her from the inside out, because what had happened the last time? She'd ended up pregnant and unmarried. Violet did not often think of her parents—the loss was too painful, even after all these years—but right now, what she wanted more than anything was her mother.

"What?"

Mac winced and Violet could almost hear him adding, *Said Violet, impulsively.*

"I would like to know more about Royal and catch up with my old friends." Something about the way Rafe said *friends* hit Violet wrong, but before she could figure out what it was, he went on, "Would you both join me for dinner tomorrow night?"

What had she done to deserve this? Because the torture of sitting through dinner with both her brother and her former lover at this exact moment of her life and pretending that nothing had changed was right up there with being stepped on by a herd of stampeding cattle.

"Well, damn," Mac said. "I'm going to be out of town. But Violet can go with you."

That was just like Mac, to assume that she spent all her free time painting her nails and listening to Backstreet Boys. She rolled her eyes at Rafe, which must not have been something people in his country did, given the way the color on his cheeks deepened.

Still, Rafe forged on, by all appearances completely unbothered by her impulsiveness or her pregnancy—except for that blush, which only made him look more sinfully handsome. Damn the man.

"Ah, that is acceptable. That way I can keep an eye on you." His gaze never wavered from hers. "Shall we meet tomorrow, say at seven?"

And Mac, the rat bastard, nodded his approval, as if they were having this entire conversation about her without remembering she was in the room.

She was totally going to blame this on hormones, this mix of rage and self-pity and the sudden urge to cry, all folded in together with desire and relief until she was so mixed up she couldn't think straight.

But had Mac already asked this man to keep an eye on her? Violet *so* did not need a babysitter at this point.

In six months or so, yes, she would need a babysitter. But before she had an actual baby, she did not. "I don't—"

"Sure, that'd be great," Mac said warmly, as if Violet were incapable of having dinner on her own without getting into some sort of trouble. "I have a meeting with Andrea scheduled that I can't get out of—Andrea's my assistant," he added, seeing Rafe's quizzical look. "But you two can go on and have a nice time."

A nice time? Oh, she had some things she wanted to say to her brother—about Rafe—but the fact was, she did actually need to talk with Rafe. Alone. "Yeah," she said, trying to sound at least a little bit excited about the prospect. Four months ago, another evening with her mystery man, Ben, would have been too good to be true. But now? "Sure. Dinner."

Rafe gave her a small smile that absolutely did not appease her. She hated him right then, because her entire world had just blown up in her face and the father of her child stood there looking as sexy as he had the night he'd taken her to bed. This pregnancy was going to change everything for her—but for him?

Yeah, they needed to talk. Preferably where no one would interrupt them to offer lemonade. "Tomorrow, then," Rafe said.

"Sounds good." Mac was staring at her, so she dug deep for something polite to say. "I look forward to it."

Rafe tilted his head down but kept his gaze locked on hers. "As do I."

"Say, Rafe, in two nights, I'll be at the Texas Cattleman's Club—we've got a meeting. If you're interested in setting down some roots locally, you could come with me."

Violet started choking. Somehow, the air had gotten

very sharp in her throat. She couldn't have heard that right—could she have? "What?"

Rafe inclined his head at Mac, but he spoke to Violet. "I have been considering branching out into the energy business, so naturally I sought out my old friend."

"Oh, naturally. That makes total sense." She tried to smile, but it must have looked more like teeth baring, because both men recoiled slightly.

Something didn't add up here. But her head was such a hot mess right now that she had no hope of figuring out what it was.

"I shall see you for dinner tomorrow night," Rafe said, and she didn't miss the particular timbre of his voice that seemed designed to send a thrill through her body. Then he turned, giving Mac a big smile that seemed less than sincere, Violet thought. "And I would be delighted to see this club of yours."

"Great," Mac said, clearly missing the forced smile. "It's a plan!"

Morning sickness was a lie. This was what Violet had concluded after a night and a day of suffering with a roiling stomach.

Of course, there was also the possibility that it was not morning sickness. A quick web search revealed that most people were only sick for the first three months, and Violet was safely in her fourth month. After all, she knew the exact date of conception.

Just thinking about that night in Ben's—Rafe's—arms again made her stomach turn. Frankly, she defied anyone to not have an upset stomach in a situation like this.

She stood in front of her meager closet in nothing but her panties and bra—her regular bra, not the black-with-white-embroidery number she'd been wearing when she met Rafe. This was a smooth white T-shirt bra. Not a danged thing sexy about it.

Because that's who she was—functional and dull and not terribly sexy. If Rafe thought she was going to show up for dinner tonight as V again, he had another think coming.

Besides, her one fancy cocktail dress—black with the lacy sleeves—well, it didn't exactly fit right now. She'd already tried it on and she couldn't get it zipped.

All those little changes her body had been experiencing—the slight weight gain, the nausea, the overwhelming urge to nap—she'd written off each and every little bump in the road as exhaustion or a bug or the changing of the seasons or stress or, hell, the phases of the moon. But now?

Not a bump in the road. A baby bump.

She had a plan. She had an appointment with an obstetrician in Holloway in two weeks. It was ridiculous that she felt she had to go to the next town over, but she hadn't exactly decided just yet on how she was going to tell Mac about this "bump in the road." She kind of had it in her mind that once she had a doctor's official…whatever, it would be easier to talk to Mac. But if she went to the local doctor in Royal, word might get back to Mac before she could gird her loins. So she was just buying a little time here.

And as for Rafe…okay, she was still working on that part of the plan. She'd done another quick internet search on his country, Al Qunfudhah. The Wikipedia article had stressed that, compared to some of the neighboring countries and kingdoms, women enjoyed a great deal of freedom in Al Qunfudhah, but the article had hit Violet funny. Why would anyone make such a big deal about women being able to drive as if it were some wondrous gift?

She did not know what Rafe intended to do. He really was, according to that same article, a sheikh. His brother ruled the country. His father had died a few years ago. But beyond that?

It had been bad enough when she'd been pregnant with some random stranger's baby. But a sheikh's baby?

She was getting ahead of herself. Dinner first. And that meant she needed to put on clothes.

She finally settled on one of her few dresses—the fanciest dress she'd owned, until she'd bought the black one on a whim. It was an olive-green cotton dress with tiny pink flowers printed on it, and it had a pink satin bow at the scoop neck. It was just a little bit girlie but also, due to the darker color, not so girlie. Plus, it was a forgiving cut and it still fit. She paired it with her jean jacket and her nice pair of brown boots, the ones with the pointed toe. She twisted her hair up and pinned it into place, but she decided against dangly earrings. This wasn't a date. This was a…negotiation, really.

That didn't stop her from putting on small hoops, as well as mascara and a little blush, though. Not enough that it looked like she was trying, but every little bit helped.

At least Mac wasn't here. If he saw her in any dress at all, he'd start asking questions. Outside of weddings and Easter services, she was not known for busting out the dresses.

She was debating the merits of her regular tinted lip balm versus actual lipstick when the doorbell rang. Crap. Violet started to hurry, but then thought better of it. She was not at Rafe's beck and call. She was pregnant. She would not hurry to accommodate him. He'd better get used to doing the accommodating around here. She slowly applied a light layer of a deep pink lipstick and then grabbed her jacket. She was cool, calm and collected. No reason to be nervous, right? Just dinner with the father of her child. Easy peasy.

But by the time she got downstairs, she was on shaky legs and it only got worse when she opened the door to find Rafe standing there, a devilish grin on his face and a single red rose in his hands. And then he took her in, her dress and her boots and her jacket, and she wished in that moment she'd tried a little harder to get the zipper up on her black dress.

"Ah," he said in a voice that sent a shiver through her. The voice was so unlike the way he'd spoken to her yesterday that she stared at him. This was the man she'd met in a bar. This was the man who'd taken her to bed.

"Hello," she said, feeling unsettled because it was so hard to reconcile this man with the one who'd sat in the living room yesterday and looked at her as if she were a deer and he were a wolf.

He still looked as though he wanted to devour her, but the difference was so startling that she was helpless to do anything but stand there, gaping.

He held out the rose. "A beautiful flower for a beautiful woman."

She couldn't help it: she wanted to kiss him again. She wanted to feel the way he'd made her feel, beautiful and sensual and desirable. But now that they knew who the other was, she didn't think chasing that little bit of happiness was the best idea. "Look—is this a date? What is this?"

There was that hardness in his expression again and she had to fight the urge to step back. She was *not* imagining that. "I would never force you to do something against your will, Violet. If you would like to go to dinner as friends, then we may do that. If you would like to consider this a more romantic evening…" His voice trailed off as his eyes warmed.

She took the rose and set it down on the foyer table. "The last time we had a romantic evening, things went wrong." Two-positive-pregnancy-tests wrong. "I think we should get a few things settled before we do anything else."

"Yes, that is a wise choice. It would be too easy to… well." She could be seeing things but he might have actually blushed. "Shall we? I made reservations at Claire's."

"Oh." Claire's was one of the nicest restaurants in town and she was wearing a jean jacket. Crap. She looked down at her outfit. "Maybe I should change?"

"You look beautiful," he said, stepping toward her. Before she could react, he had cupped her chin in his hand and lifted her face. "You were beautiful that night and you are beautiful now. And anyone who would deign to criticize you will face my wrath."

Wow, that was the sexiest-sounding threat she'd ever heard. Violet was speechless. Even if she could talk, she had no idea what might come out of her mouth. Something impulsive? Something stupid? Both?

Or, worse, would she tell him how much she'd missed him, how much she'd savored their night together?

Because it would be terrible for him to back her into this house and carry her up the stairs the way he'd carried her down the hall of his hotel. It would be awful if he laid her out on her own bed and did all those things he'd done before.

Yup. It would simply be the worst.

"Ah," he breathed, so close to her that she could have tilted her head just a little and brought her lips against his, "you asked me what this evening is about. But now I ask you—what is it you want this evening to be?"

Violet was used to dealing with men. She did a man's work, day in and day out. She dealt with cowboys and her brother, and didn't spend a hell of a lot of time in a beauty salon, gossiping with other women. She could more than hold her own when some jerk got it into his head that she, a delicate female, shouldn't be fixing fences or branding cattle or any of those manly things men liked to think they were the only ones capable of getting done. Men who decided they were alphas and she had to fall into line either got their metaphorical butts handed to them on a platter or a black eye as a souvenir of the experience.

So, really, Violet should not have felt this urge to give in to Rafe, to tell him that whatever he wanted, she wanted. But she was tempted. The masculinity coming off him was so strong, so potent, it was almost as if she could see the air shimmering around him, like heat off a highway.

All those men before—they'd been all talk. They had to tell people they were the boss because otherwise, no one else would know it. But Rafe? Jesus, he was in a different class. This was not just an alpha man, this was a man born to power, a man who breathed it as easily as he breathed air.

This was a sheikh. *Her* sheikh.

But just as she was about to succumb to his sheer machismo, she remembered their situation.

So she forced herself to lift her chin out of his grasp and she forced herself to stare into his eyes—dark and warm and waiting on her to say the word so he could strip her right out of her dress—and she said, "I want to figure out how we got here and what we're going to do next." Dang it all, her voice came out as something closer to sultry than businesslike.

Rafe heard it, too, and his lips curved into a knowing

smile. "Ah, yes. How we got here. I seem to recall carrying a beautiful, mysterious woman to my room and—"

"No, stop." Heat flushed her body, but she was not going to fall for him a second time. She had enough going on right now. "I mean more along the lines of what happened afterward. I'm pregnant. We need to be taking this seriously."

That worked. Rafe straightened and, sighing, nodded. "Would you like to discuss this over dinner or somewhere more private?"

Private was good. Private was great. But private also meant more of those smoldering looks and hot touches from this man and again, she was totally going to blame the hormones on this one, but she didn't know how strong she could be if she had to fend off those sorts of advances all evening long. "Dinner," she said decisively.

Rafe, to his credit, didn't use all of his innate power to overrule her, just as he hadn't coerced her into doing anything she hadn't wanted that night. Instead, with a nod of his head that veered closer to a bow of respect than anything else, he said, "Dinner, then."

Three

Rafe and Violet were shown to a secluded table tucked into a small alcove in the back of the restaurant. Perfect.

He needed this dinner to be in the public eye because he had little doubt that word of it would make its way back to Mac, and Rafe wanted everyone to see him acting like a gentleman. But he also needed to be hidden away enough that he and Violet could discuss things like pregnancy and plans without being overheard.

He held Violet's chair for her, which gave him the opportunity to admire her from the back. There'd been a moment earlier this evening when he'd wanted nothing more than to sweep her off her feet and carry her to a bedroom. Any bedroom would do. In this outfit, she was not the seductress V had been all those months ago, but she was also not the angry cowgirl who, just yesterday, had informed him she was carrying his child.

Yesterday, she had not been so very hard to resist,

between her shell-shocked appearance and her perhaps justifiable anger. But today?

As she sat, Rafe had to physically restrain himself from leaning down and pressing his lips against the exposed nape of her neck, right next to where a tendril of hair had escaped her updo and lay curled against her fair skin like an invitation.

He managed not to kiss her there, but he must have stood too still for too long, for Violet turned and looked up over her shoulder at him and said, "Yes?"

Rafe didn't answer immediately. He took his time circling the table and taking his seat. "I do not think I have told you how glad I am to see you again."

Violet notched an eyebrow at him. "Seriously? You didn't act all that glad yesterday."

"True. But I think that, given the surprising nature of our reunion, we can both be forgiven for being less than enthusiastic at first."

Her eyes narrowed and he got the feeling he'd said the wrong thing. "Oh, really?"

This called for a tactical retreat. A fast one. "Let us plan, as you have requested. How long have you been aware of your impending blessing?"

Because he needed to know that she was being honest—that not only was she expecting, but that it was his child. The four months between that evening and this one left plenty of time for her to have taken other lovers.

Her cheeks colored. "Well, since yesterday. I was in the process of peeing on a stick when Mac came to tell me you were in the living room."

Rafe coughed over her coarse language, which made her eyes narrow again. "I did not realize," he said. "Just… yesterday?"

"Yes." After a pause, she said, "I had been feeling a

little off for a while—super tired all the time, gaining a little weight. I had thought maybe I just had a stomach bug that was hanging on, but then my friend Clare started asking about how I was feeling and suggested…" She swallowed, staring at her water glass. "And I bought a test. A three-pack, just in case, you know?"

"I see," he said, although he was not entirely sure he did. "How many tests were positive?"

"Two. I didn't believe the first one. But two that said the same thing…" Her voice trailed off sadly. "I guess I was maybe a little rude yesterday, but I had gone from suddenly realizing I was pregnant and wondering how the heck I was ever going to find you and tell you, to walking into the living room and finding you. Except you weren't who you said you were."

"Yes," he said sympathetically. "I can see why that would have been a bit of a shock. It was quite unexpected to see you again."

She wrinkled her nose. "Why did you say your name was Ben that night?"

This was dangerous territory because the truth would endanger his scheme. So he turned her question back on her. "Why did you go by V?"

She did not answer immediately and then, just as she opened her mouth to respond, the server came up to take their orders. Rafe did not often drink. In fact, he had not drunk wine since that night. Perhaps that was why he had taken V to bed, because his inhibitions had been lowered.

But tonight, he decided he needed a glass of wine to get through this evening. Otherwise, he might overreact the way he had to Violet's announcement yesterday and if he enraged her again, it would put his whole scheme in danger of collapsing.

He did not know if Violet was his friend or his enemy.

What she was, at this point, was a former lover, and those relationships could go either way. But no matter how this played out, Rafe knew he needed to keep her close.

So he ordered a bottle of sauvignon blanc to accompany his filet mignon and her chicken dish. In the past several months, he had grown quite fond of Texas beef. Even the barbecue was delicious and quite unlike the way beef was prepared in his country.

But when he placed their orders, Violet narrowed those beautiful eyes at him again. It was only when the server was safely out of earshot that she leaned forward and said in a tense whisper, "I can't drink."

"Oh?"

"Because I'm pregnant?" she said, although it was clearly not a question. "I'm not supposed to drink." A look of panic flared over her face. "Do you know anything about pregnancy? About babies?"

Rafe rolled his hand. "Of course not. I do not have any children and, if I did, we would have nannies to care for them. That is how I was raised."

Had he thought this declaration would relieve her anxiety? If so, he had guessed wrong. The color drained out of her face and, if anything, she looked more worried than before. "Nannies? As in, plural? I didn't—I mean, that's not what I had been thinking for our child."

"Let us not get ahead of ourselves," he cautioned, because that look of terror on her face made him strangely uncomfortable. He should be reveling in her panic—thrilled, even, that he was striking such a blow against Mac's sister. This was revenge at its finest.

And yet, it wasn't. If her pleasure had once been his, her terror was also his. It was a weakness he did not like because weaknesses could be exploited.

"Okay," she said softly.

"Let us start at the beginning," he went on, more gently than he had planned to. But it worked because she took a deep breath and sat back in her chair, looking almost calm. "I did not realize who you were that night. And I assume, based on your statement earlier that you were wondering how you'd find me, you did not know who I was?"

"No, I didn't. No names. That was the deal." She cleared her throat and began to fiddle with her silverware, arranging the knife and the fork in perfect alignment. "I was V for the same reason I was out in Holloway instead of Royal. I wanted a night out where word wouldn't get back to Mac." She looked up and he could see in her eyes that she was pleading with him. "He wants what's best for me, I know that. But sometimes…he can be suffocating. I mean, he doesn't think this is a date because he asked you to keep an eye on me, didn't he?"

"This is true," Rafe confirmed.

She exhaled heavily. "That's how he is. Every man is either a threat to my innocence or a babysitter."

"But you have reached your maturity," Rafe noted. "You are not the same little sister he told me about when we were in university twelve years ago."

She snorted. "Try telling him that. He still treats me like I'm sixteen and lost without my parents. But I'm not. I'm a grown woman now and I'm capable of running half the family business and…okay, so getting pregnant wasn't my finest hour, but I can do this, Rafe."

Rafe thought this over as the wine was served. Violet asked for a Sprite instead. "I must ask—your innocence?"

"Lord," Violet said, rolling her eyes toward the ceiling, and Rafe couldn't tell if she was praying for strength or something else. "Fine. No, I was not a virgin. You?"

Rafe almost glared at her because this line of questioning was not something sheikhs had to endure. But as she watched him, he quickly realized that, to Violet, he was not primarily a sheikh. He was, first and foremost, a man to whom she would be forever tied. "No. And before you ask, I am not currently seeing anyone else. In fact, except for our evening together, I have been celibate for some time."

Her lips quirked into something that was almost a smile. "Celibate, huh?"

He shrugged, trying to keep it casual. "I have been busy. My brother is the sheikh of Al Qunfudhah and I run the shipping business owned by our family. While our sheikhdom was originally founded on oil, we have diversified and my shipping business now accounts for thirty percent of the gross domestic product."

"But celibate? You're a sheikh," she said, clearly puzzled. Then her gaze drifted over his face, his shoulders, and down his chest before she looked back at him. "And you're gorgeous."

Rafe felt his face warm. "So I have been told. But just because I could have any woman I want does not mean I should."

"And modest," she added in a mocking tone. But she smiled when she said it. "That's a refreshing attitude, I have to tell you. Most men would take whatever they could get."

"I am not 'most men.'"

"No," she agreed, her smile warming. "You're not."

Rafe was pleased. He should have been pleased because Violet was opening up to him and the more he drew her in, the more complete his revenge would be.

But that was not why he leaned forward and placed his hand on top of hers, stilling it in the middle of adjusting the precise placement of her soup spoon. "And you? Are you involved with anyone?"

"No," she said in a breathy whisper. "Most guys don't last too long before my brother scares them off."

"That must be frustrating."

She tried to shrug off both the sentiment and his hand and, given that they were in public, he had no choice but to sit back in his seat. "It is, but it's also a blessing—I guess. If they can't stand up to Mac, how could I expect them to stand next to me, you know?"

Rafe thought about this. He knew, without a shadow of a doubt, that standing against Mac would not be problematic. "Indeed."

Their meals arrived along with Violet's soda. She sipped at it gingerly and took small bites of her food. "Is it all right?" he asked, concerned. If she was expecting, shouldn't she be eating more?

"It's fine. I just—well, I've been dealing with morning sickness—which is a lie, by the way. My stomach's most upset in the evening. And for a lot of people, it ends after the third month, but I think it's actually getting worse."

This news was alarming. "Have you seen a doctor yet? Do you think everything is all right?"

She looked at him, trying not to smile and not quite succeeding. "I'm fine. According to the internet, this is all normal. I scheduled an appointment with a doctor in Holloway and the quickest they could get me in was in two weeks."

He set his knife and fork down a bit harder than he meant to, given how the beverages danced in their glasses and Violet's eyes widened. "That is not soon enough. I can have a private doctor here tomorrow—Friday at the latest."

"Rafe," she said, her soft Texas accent caressing

his name like a lover's hands. She'd said *Ben* that way, but not *Rafe*. Not like that. It was enough to make him pause as he typed in the password to his phone. "It's fine. There's no danger."

"I merely want what is best for you and the child," he said, his voice getting caught somewhere in the back of his throat. And he was surprised to realize how very much he meant it.

"Yeah," she said in that quiet voice, "about that. Okay, so I'm not seeing anyone and you're not either. Which doesn't mean that we're together."

"I would not make such presumptions," he assured her.

"It just means that, for once, there's one less complication to deal with."

"Agreed. And I would not be outside of bounds if I asked you to refrain from starting a relationship with anyone else while you are carrying my child, would I?"

What started out as a smile progressed into a full giggle. There was simply no other word for it. Violet McCallum was giggling at him. "Out of bounds. Not outside."

He should have been insulted that she was mocking him. What was it about this woman that made him not only accept her teasing, but crave it? "Ah, I see. Thank you. I shall remember 'out of bounds' in the future."

"No," she said, wiping a tear from her eye. "You are not out of bounds. Dating is a challenge in the best of times. Right now, I can't see how it'd be anything but impossible. I am not looking to start a relationship right now."

A new thought occurred to him as Violet settled down and sipped her soda. Rafe's original plan, once he had realized that Violet was V, was to use and discard Violet much as Mac had done to Nasira. That was the ultimate revenge, a sister's honor for a sister's honor.

But now that Rafe was spending more time with Violet, he wondered if he would actually be able to do that to her. She was, after all, carrying his child—if she could be believed. And Rafe desperately wanted to believe her.

What if, instead of treating Mac's beloved little sister as Mac himself had treated Nasira, Rafe instead just *took* Violet? Not a kidnapping—nothing so brutish as that—but Mac had dedicated the past twelve years of his life to protecting his sister. If Rafe were to marry the mother of his child and move her far away, would that not be avenging his family's honor—while preserving his own bloodline? Violet was already tired of Mac and his interference in her life. It would not be that difficult to turn her against her brother completely.

This was an idea that had much merit.

"That is good," he said, trying to keep his voice level. "We should come to an agreement upon what is best for the child."

He must not have kept his voice as level as he would have liked, for Violet's eyes widened. "That sounds..."

He put on his best smile, his American smile. He did not smile like this at home. He had no need for it. But here, in Texas, this situation required finesse. It was tempting to just tell her they would get married and that she would bear his child and live in Al Qunfudhah. If he were at home, that is all he would have to do.

But Violet was not one of his people, and he knew enough about her to know that any such broad proclamation would have the opposite effect. Violet would refuse and, as long as she was in Texas, she *could* continue to refuse him. That was her legal right in this country, he was reasonably sure.

He would ask Nolan, but his lawyer was no longer his lawyer and, at times like this, Rafe missed the man's counsel. He wished mightily that Nolan had not quit Rafe's employ because he had fallen for a local woman—a woman with another man's child, no less. It had been another betrayal, one that stung.

It did not matter. He had promised he would not force Violet to do something she did not wish to do and he would keep that promise, for the sake of his child if for no other reason.

No, what he needed to do was convince her that she wanted to marry him. It should not be difficult. They were attracted to each other and they already had electric chemistry together. All he had to do was push that electric attraction and make her love him.

In the back of his head, he heard the severe voice of his father berating him. There had never been a time when the sheikh had not told Rafe what a worthless son and worthless brother he was. His father had held Rafe personally responsible for the loss of Nasira's innocence and Rafe had been punished accordingly. He had not been allowed to finish his American university studies. He had not been allowed to live abroad. He had been forcibly returned to Al Qunfudhah and confined to the basement of the family compound like a dog that had to be broken. Nasira, at least, had escaped into a marriage that suited her. But not Rafe.

Much like his siblings, Rafe was supposed to have been married off to a bride of his father's choosing, the daughter of another warlord or royal. The marriage would further cement Al Qunfudhah's position in the Middle East, and a suitable bride would bring honor to the bin Saleed bloodlines.

But after Nasira had been compromised by the one man Rafe trusted with his very life, Rafe's father had refused to allow Rafe the escape of marriage. Nasira had been ruined, so their father had not cared when she had married an Englishman and left the country. For all intents and purposes, Nasira had been dead to the old sheikh. Rafe had not been so lucky. He had been stuck in a hell that was not entirely his own making. The only thought that had sustained him during those first years was that of exacting his revenge on Mac McCallum.

It had been a relief for all of them when his father had died.

Now, years after the man's death, Rafe could hear his ominous voice again. *A true sheikh does not play games. A true sheikh would not concern himself with the wants of a woman. A true sheikh would have already carried this woman back to Al Qunfudhah and put her in a harem.*

Not that the bin Saleeds had harems. They did not. But in times past, the sheikh would have kept many women as his concubines. It had always been Rafe's opinion that his father lamented this cultural loss more than anything else.

"You got quiet there," Violet said, pushing what was left of her meal around her plate.

"I was thinking," he said truthfully. "There is something of a cultural gap between us that we need to bridge. My child will be a bin Saleed and I would like him—"

"Or her," Violet interjected.

Rafe let a grin play over his mouth. "Or her," he amended, "to know our people and our ways."

Violet frowned slightly, as if he had once again said something out of place. "I was trying to do a little reading on your people. The article I read made it sound like Al Qunfundaha—"

Now it was his turn to correct her. "Al Qunfudhah."

"Yeah, I'm probably going to screw that up a few more times," she said, forcing a smile onto her face. "But—I mean, what I'm trying to say is, what I've read makes it sound like your country is trying to be progressive toward women and minority rights but…it's still not like it is here."

What was she talking about? Rafe gave her a look and she threw her hands up. "I'm not making sense, am I?"

"Not entirely." He followed this up with another warm smile. This time, it was not as forced. Perhaps the wine was loosening him up. "But you are concerned about your place and the place of our child in my country, no?"

"No—wait, I mean yes. That's exactly what I'm concerned about. I'm not this world traveler like you are. I've hardly left Texas. I was supposed to follow Mac and go to Harvard, but then my parents died and we had to run the business and…" She smiled again, and Rafe thought it looked like an apology. It was. "I'm sorry. I'm just trying to process everything that's happened and I'm hormonal and you're being wonderfu,l but I'm making a fool of myself—again—and it's still a lot."

He was being wonderful? He should not be pleased with this statement. But he was.

He leaned forward and cupped her face. Her eyes widened but she didn't pull away as she had earlier. Instead, she leaned into his touch. Her skin was soft as silk against his palm, but warmer. "Ah, I am the only fool here."

She looked up at him, her eyes wide and deep and beautiful. "You are?"

"I am." Dimly, he was aware he was leaning in, that her face—her lips—were getting closer. "I find I wish to give you anything your heart desires. Tell me, what is it you want?"

She looked down at her dish. "I like it here. This is my life. But I am so tired of living with Mac, you know?

There's a ranch to the north of us—the Wild Aces. The Double M is leasing it because our water supply got compromised in the tornado, but I wanted to buy it outright. It's a beautiful piece of land and the house on the property is almost a hundred years old—one of those grand old homes. I've always loved it." She looked up at him with much confidence in her eyes. Rafe was certain her bravado was not entirely honest. "If I'm going to have a family—and that does seem to be the plan—I'd love to have my own house, my own land."

"The Wild Aces, you say?" He said it as if he had never heard of such a place before but, in truth, he knew exactly where the property was. The owner had been reluctant to sell to Nolan in large part because she was leasing the water to the Double M. Unlike many of their neighbors, she already had a steady stream of secondary income and was not as tempted by Samson Oil's generous offer.

But the Wild Aces was key to his scheme. If he owned that land, he owned the Double M's water supply. And if he owned that, he owned Mac McCallum. His revenge would be complete and nothing could stop him.

Nothing except a beautiful woman who was carrying his child. "You wish to have this land as your own?"

"I tried to get Mac to buy it, but he always reacts to one of my ideas the same way he reacted back when we were kids—oh, isn't that cute, Violet's trying to think like a big girl!" she said in the high-pitched, nasal voice many Americans used when speaking to small children and animals. Then she rolled her eyes. "It's so frustrating. I have to come at him sideways. He'll at least consider any idea his assistant brings up, so I have to ask Andrea to ask Mac. If I bring it up, he shoots it down, like I'm not smart enough to make wise business decisions on my own."

This was at odds with the way Mac had described Violet's management of the Double M, but Rafe did not show his confusion. "And if you had this land, you would raise our child on it?"

He was very careful not to make it a promise, because he was a man of his word and if he did something foolish like promise Violet the Wild Aces, he would be honor bound to keep that promise and that would mean all of his work was for naught.

Besides, he had no intention of staying in Royal or any part of Texas. And being Mac's neighbor? Out of the question. Rafe had to convince Violet that she belonged with him and that they belonged in Al Qunfudhah.

But making Violet think he would do something so grand as buy her a ranch without actually promising to do so—well, that was tailor-made to his scheme, wasn't it?

"I would love that," she said, her face lighting up with joy.

So much joy, in fact, that Rafe was horrified to hear himself say, "I will see what I can do." Which was not the same as promising her the ranch. He had merely promised to investigate it. He was still operating with honor.

"Really?" Her eyes were wide and she was looking at him with what he could only describe as adoration. "You'd do that for me?"

He had lost control of the situation—of himself—that much was clear. And it became clearer when he said, "I would."

"Rafe..."

And he was powerless to do anything but lean forward, to bring himself closer to her, to see how she looked at him. To be the man she saw, not the man he was. "Violet…"

"Will there be anything else?"

At the sound of the server's voice, Rafe shook himself back to his senses. Had he really been about to kiss Violet? In public? In the middle of this restaurant?

Yes. Yes, he had been. Which was not a part of the plan. He was here as a chaperone to Violet, not a seducer. "No, that will be all," he said, his voice harder than he meant it to be. The server left the bill and hurried off.

Rafe glanced at the bottle of wine—he had consumed perhaps two glasses, at most. This was the problem with abstaining from both women and wine for so long. His tolerance for both was quite low.

"Come," he said, paying the bill with cash. "I shall take you home."

Four

What she would *give* to be able to read this man. That was what occupied Violet's thoughts as she rode in Rafe's very nice sports car. Because he shifted between hard and soft and cold and warm and—yeah, she was going to say it—scary and sexy so fast that she was getting whiplash just watching him.

"This land is quite beautiful," he said conversationally.

Right now was a perfect example. Minutes ago, he'd leaned over and touched her face and told her he wanted to give her whatever she wanted—no, that wasn't right. He wanted to give her *her heart's desires*.

That was the man she'd spent the night with four months ago—sensual and sexy and whispering sweet nothings to her.

But then the waitress had interrupted them—which was good because if word got back to Mac that Rafe had been on the verge of kissing her in public, things would have gotten ugly fast—and all that sensual goodness had flipped off like a switch and suddenly Violet was sitting with an ice-cold man who had terrified the waitress with a few words and a hard look.

Violet didn't know which version of Rafe was in this car with her. But she did know that she vastly preferred the sexy sheikh to the domineering one.

The silence in this car—this very, very nice car that was probably a Lamborghini or a Maserati or some other exclusive brand of vehicle that was expensive and rare and designed to throw other men into a jealous rage—was deafening. She didn't belong here. Not in this fancy sports car, not with a sheikh.

She was just Violet McCallum. Nothing really that special here. She got crap on her boots every day and she was pregnant. Big freaking whoop.

Except…except when Rafe looked at her and spoke to her with that voice of sunshine. She almost felt as if she could do anything she wanted. *Be* anyone she wanted. Which was exactly how she'd gotten into this fine mess in the first place.

He wanted to give her whatever she wanted. Well, what did she want? She knew the answer to that—she wanted the same kind of happy family for her child that she'd grown up with. She'd told him about the Wild Aces—but did she want him there with her? Did she want to go to his country—even if she went as a member of the royal family?

It was all too much, too soon. She wasn't going to do anything stupid like marry Rafe. First things first. Soon she'd be a mother. Which would be wonderful, she had to admit. Now that she and Rafe were getting a few things straight, she was starting to feel more excited about this new adventure. She'd loved her mother—both of her parents, of course, but Violet and her mother had always had a special relationship.

"Now it is you who is silent," Rafe said and thank God, he didn't sound regal about it. "What is the saying? A dollar for your thoughts?"

She grinned, feeling some of her tension melting. "A penny. But you were close!"

Rafe tilted his head in her direction. "I assure you, your thoughts are worth far more than a penny. Do not undervalue yourself."

Coming from anyone else, it would have sounded like a load of manure. And maybe it still was. But the way the words rolled off Rafe's tongue…

"I was just thinking of my mother."

"Ah," he said softly, but he didn't barge into the silence as Mac did every single time Violet had tried to talk about their parents.

Her brother had always had some statement ready to go about how her grief was normal and they were going to get through this together and she was going to be *just fine*. Then, before she could get a danged word in edgewise, he'd pull her into a bear hug and tell her how proud he was of her and how he was going to take care of her and then he'd hurry out of the room, as if she didn't know his eyes were watering. As if they weren't allowed to have feelings in front of each other.

Instead of telling her how she was supposed to feel, Rafe waited for her to talk.

How weird was that?

"I was sixteen when the plane crashed," she said simply. "But I assume you know that?"

"Yes," he replied.

"I mean, I still miss them, but it's been twelve years. Bad things happen and people move on. Or we try," she added, thinking of Mac's overbearing version of love. "But this pregnancy—I was just thinking how much I'd like my mom to be here for this. If that makes sense." If anyone could talk Violet through an unplanned pregnancy, it'd have been Mom.

They'd had their share of fights—Violet had been a teenager, after all. But she'd always known her mom would be there for her. Until she wasn't.

"You were close to your mother?"

What an odd question. "Isn't everyone?"

"Ah," Rafe said, and the regretful tone in his voice made Violet glance over at him. He looked pained—not as though she'd kicked him in the shins, but a deeper pain that spoke of a lifetime of loneliness.

"Oh, right," she hurried to say, remembering what he'd said earlier. "Nannies. I'm sorry."

"I will, of course, defer to you," he said in a not-at-all seductive voice. He sounded more like a businessman and she didn't particularly like it. "If you wish to be more involved, then by all means, I will make that happen."

"How?"

"Excuse me?"

"How?" she repeated. "Look, my life is here. I run the family ranch. I know you told Mac you'd go with him to the meeting at the Texas Cattleman's Club because you were thinking of relocating but honestly? I don't know what your plans are. I don't know why you're here now and I don't know when you'll be leaving. I don't..." Her words trailed off and she suddenly felt like a teenager again, so sure of everything when, in reality, she knew very little. "I don't want to move to the Middle East. Even if your country is progressive."

"I see." Rafe pulled into the driveway of the Double

M. "I can safely say that my plans have recently been revised."

"You want this baby? I mean..." she quickly corrected, because all of a sudden an image of Rafe carrying her child onto an airplane while Violet stood in the terminal, watching them go—powerless to stop them—oh, God. No. "What I'm saying is, you want me to have this baby? Because I want to keep the baby."

"The child will be a bin Saleed. Of course I want you to have the baby," he said with a significant edge to his voice. "I will, of course, need independent verification that I am the father."

"What?" The word rushed out of her like that one time when a bucking calf had caught her in the gut with a hoof. "You don't believe me?"

"I do believe you," he said, the honey back in his voice. "We were together and I can only guess that, at some point, the condoms failed. I did use them because I gave you my word I would. But clearly, something went wrong and my brother, the sheikh of Al Qunfudhah—he will not be satisfied taking the word of an American woman. If the child is to have all the rights and privileges of the bin Saleed family, we must prove that I am the legitimate father."

"Oh." She hadn't considered that. She'd been so focused on what Mac would do when he found out that she hadn't considered Rafe's family obligations.

A family of sheikhs at that. "What will your brother do? When he finds out?"

Rafe slid a sideways smile at her. It was not terribly reassuring. "Calm yourself, my dear. Fareed is not my father and I am no longer powerless. He will most likely insist that the child be cared for and raised to honor our traditions, but," he added with what could only be described as a twinkle in his eye, "I do not think this will spark an international incident."

There was something there, something just below the surface of what he'd said that tugged at her consciousness. But she had a more pressing question she needed answered before she tried to unpack what he'd really meant. "Will you want custody?"

That's what she said. What she meant was, *Will you take my baby away from me?*

Rafe pulled up next to the ranch house and parked before answering. "Ah, yes. We must work out an agreement. This is why my plans have changed. I do not want to be away from my flesh and blood for too long."

So, yes, it was an odd way to phrase it. But the sentiment was what she needed to hear. He wouldn't take her baby and disappear in the middle of a different continent. "Okay, good. I know you said you were interested in expanding into energy—are you thinking of living in Royal? At least part of the time?"

He regarded her for what felt like an eternity. "I am thinking of many things," he said, his voice low. So low, in fact, that she had to lean forward to catch all of his words. "But if I stay here—even part of the time—we would have to have an...understanding, if you will."

"What kind of understanding?"

His gaze traced her face and she felt her cheeks warm. "I know we have agreed not to see other people while you are expecting, but I do not know how I could be around you and see you with another man. It would cut me," he added, placing his hand over his heart.

"Oh," she breathed. What was he saying? If he stayed in Royal, he'd expect them to be a couple? Together? "You mean...what do you mean?" Because if he meant that they were to live together—or get married—she didn't know how she was supposed to feel about that. Panic? Yeah, that was an option. Panic was always a good backup. She was barely coping with being pregnant—how was she supposed to throw a marriage into that mix?

But then another thought occurred to her. Because the one physical thing she hadn't gotten out of Rafe the first time they were together was waking up in his arms. That wouldn't be a hardship, falling asleep with Rafe by her side every night and waking up with him every morning.

Rafe's gaze was burning her in the best way possible. There was so much going on in his eyes—which was at least something to go off, as he was otherwise completely unreadable. Then he reached over and picked up her hand, leaning into her space to press his lips against the back of it. "I have not stopped thinking of you since our night of passion, Violet. I cannot tell you how many times I almost went searching for you. You…" He looked up at her, his voice raw. "You have graced my dreams and haunted my waking hours, a ghost of a woman I could see, but not touch. And it has been torture. The sweetest torture I've ever known."

Oh, my. Was he serious? God, how she wanted to believe he was, that their night together had been more than a one-night stand. "I thought of you, too. I…I still have your note."

He hadn't let her hand go. He was still holding it close to his mouth, where she could feel the warmth of his breath against her skin. Oh, that smile—all of her panic about the future dimmed in the light of his smile. God, Rafe was such a handsome man. "I am pleased to hear that. But I had made a promise to you—one night, no names—and I was honor bound to keep my promise. So I did not search for you. I did not try. I accepted my fate—that one night with my beautiful, mysterious V was all

I would get. And now I have this opportunity to know you—not just as V, but as a woman. As Violet. This is a second chance. I would be a fool to let this—to let you—slip through my fingers a second time."

"Oh, Rafe." She had never heard such a romantic speech in her life—and she'd certainly never been the subject of one. "Is that what you want? A real relationship?"

He turned her hand over and kissed her palm. "I want many things. But you are the one who carries the child. It is you who must be satisfied first." When he looked at her again, she felt as if she were falling into his eyes and she might never want to climb back out. "I think it is time for you to tell me what *you* want."

The air between them suddenly felt very warm, and she had a flashback to the way he'd bought her a drink at the bar at the Holloway Inn and then joined her. At some point between the first drink and the third, he'd leaned over and said those exact words to her. *I think it is time for you to tell me what you want.*

And what she'd wanted then was to be swept off her feet. She'd wanted to have fun; she'd wanted to feel beautiful and special. She'd wanted to be wanted because she was Violet, not because of her brother or her family name or her ranch. Just her.

And she said to him now what she'd said to him on that night. "Why don't we talk about this someplace else?"

One dark eyebrow notched up. "Are you inviting me in?"

She looked back at the dark ranch house. Mac was gone for the next two nights. She knew it. Rafe knew it. She had the run of the place.

"We're not done talking," she said. Although she

wasn't speaking loudly, her voice filled the small space between them.

"Indeed, we are not."

Violet started to undo her seat belt but before she could get her door open, Rafe was out of the car and hurrying around to her side. "Allow me," he said in that honey-and-sunshine voice as he opened her door and extended a hand to her.

She let him pull her to her feet, but he didn't let go of her. Only a few inches separated them. Despite the spring breeze, Violet could feel the warmth of his chest.

"This is just to talk," she heard herself say. "This doesn't mean anything else." Which was possibly the most pointless thing she'd ever said in the history of talking because of course Rafe's coming into her empty home meant something. It might even mean everything.

"I would make no such presumptions," he readily agreed. But his words were directly at odds with the way his thumb was now stroking over her knuckles. She was reading him now, loud and clear. "So tell me what it is you want. What are your dreams for the future? What part do you want me to play?"

"You're being too perfect," she told him. Because it was the truth. Everything he was saying—everything he was doing—was exactly what she needed, when she needed it.

He tilted his head to one side. "Has no one ever asked you what you want?"

"Oh, sure. What do I want for dinner, whether we should castrate the calves today or tomorrow, that sort of thing."

Well, that was some award-winning conversation right there. But Rafe was caressing her hand and looking down at her exactly the way he had when he'd pinned her in an elevator four months ago. Yeah, her mouth and her brain weren't exactly operating on the same wavelength at this point. Heat poured through her body, loosening her limbs as she melted into him, and all she wanted was for him to pick her up and carry her into that house.

"A crime, to be certain," Rafe murmured, cupping her face with his other hand. "I am asking you now. Tell me what you want."

He lifted her face and gazed deeply into her eyes and she was right where she'd been four months ago. She shouldn't do this. She shouldn't have done it last time. She should push Rafe back and cross her legs at the ankle and try, for once, to be the prim and proper sort of girl who was absolutely not swayed by a beautiful man with a beautiful voice.

Rafe was not going to let her go, though. He leaned in closer, so close she felt his breath on her lips, and said, "Because what you want is what I want."

And she didn't want to push him away any more than she had wanted to push him away in the elevator. In his arms, all those months ago, she hadn't been Mac's little sister and she hadn't yet been a future mother. For one glorious night, she'd been who she wanted to be.

It wasn't wrong to be that—to be herself. She could do that with Rafe—and only Rafe.

"Kiss me," she said.

His lips curved into a smile—one that warmed her from the inside out. "Are you sure? Because when it comes to you, I do not know if one kiss will ever be enough."

"I'm sure," she whispered, making her decision. "So kiss me."

Five

Judging from the way Violet threw her arms around his neck and pulled him down roughly into a searing kiss, this was all going perfectly according to his revised scheme. Making Violet fall in love with him would be an easy task. All he had to give her was exactly what she wanted—and, as far as he could tell, what she wanted was a passionate lover and freedom from her overbearing brother. Those were two requirements he could meet easily.

But any thought of revenge went flying out the window as Violet's tongue traced his lips. He had not lied to her—his thoughts had rarely been far from her and to suddenly find her back in his arms was almost more than he could bear.

"Violet," he groaned against the delicate skin of her neck. "Are you quite sure?"

"I want you," she said, her voice practically a growl, which sent an uncharacteristic shiver down his spine.

This was why he had not been able to put Violet from his thoughts—she made him do things that were out of character, such as kiss his enemy's sister because he wanted to do nothing but feel her body against his.

He lifted her against his straining erection and began carrying her toward her house. Every step drove him against her soft heat and there were no thoughts of revenge. There was only this burning need to bury himself in Violet's body, to make her cry out with pleasure.

When they got to the ranch house, he set her down and turned her around so she could open the door. And if she couldn't get it open, he'd break it down. Anything to get inside. But as she fumbled with her keys, the situation grew dire. "Violet," he groaned.

She finally managed to get the door open and then they were safely inside, away from any accidental witnesses. He pulled her back against him, letting her feel what she did to him. "Your room," he whispered against the base of her neck.

"This way." She pulled away and he let her go just enough that she could lead him up the stairs, but he couldn't keep his hands off of her. He traced the outline of her bottom through the thin cotton of her dress, which made her giggle.

When she cleared the top stair, and Rafe was certain they wouldn't tumble to their doom, he gathered her in his arms. All at once she was kissing him and he was kissing her back and pushing her jacket off her shoulders. Dimly, he thought he should be going more slowly, taking his time to savor her—her taste, the small noises she made when he did something she liked.

But he could not take his time. He needed her right now.

He tried to back her toward the right, where an open

door beckoned with the promise of a bed, but she corrected their course and led him left. Then her fingers began to work at the buttons on his shirt as she walked backward into her room.

At least he assumed it was her room. It was dominated by an enormous canopy bed with four tall posts holding up a drape of sheer light blue fabric.

"Kiss me," she said again, grabbing his face in her hands and pulling it down. "Please, Rafe, please."

"I cannot refuse you," he said, carrying her toward the bed. In one swift motion, he peeled her dress off and she was nearly bare before him.

Her hands stilled against his chest. "I've changed. Since that night." She said it as if she were afraid of what his reaction to her body would be.

But Rafe was staring down at the luscious curves. "If anything, you have changed for the better." He lifted her hands away from his chest and guided her back onto the bed until she lay before him. He could not be so thoughtless as to take her roughly, not when she was already nervous. Their first time, she had shared the wine with him and there had been no hesitation. But this time, he knew he needed to reassure her.

"Oh, Rafe," she moaned as he kissed down her neck to the valley between her breasts. Yes, he thought that perhaps they were slightly larger—fuller, he decided as he cupped them in his hands and slid his thumbs over the cups of the bra, right where her nipples should be.

"Take it off," she whispered, threading her hands through his hair and lifting herself up off the bed.

"Your wish is my command," he said, reaching behind her back and deftly removing her bra.

"If anyone else said that to me, I'd think they were full of it," she giggled. "But when you say it..."

"It is because I mean it." He lowered his head to her breast, letting his tongue work her nipple into a stiff peak. "I cannot help myself," he murmured against her skin as he moved to her other breast. "When I'm with you…"

"I know. I feel the same way. I—oh!" That was as far as she got before Rafe kissed his way lower, pulling her innocent white panties down until she was completely exposed to him.

After that, there were no more words to be said because he was busy bringing her to the heights of pleasure with his mouth and she was busy moaning and writhing under his touch. She kept her hands buried in his hair, guiding him in the direction that she most needed him to go.

Their first time, she had climaxed when he slipped his finger inside her. He would hate for her to think that he had forgotten what she liked best, so he repeated the move.

"Rafe!" she cried out as he lapped at her body, her inner muscles tightening around his finger.

And he could not wait anymore, not for her. He could not even do this properly and remove all of his clothing. He unbuckled his pants and grabbed the condom out of his back pocket and somehow managed to get the thing rolled on before he was against her, covering her body with his as he thrust into her warmth.

"Violet," he groaned, wanting to hold himself back—to hold himself apart from her because that was the smart thing to do, the calculated move that would contain whatever emotional havoc she wreaked. But he couldn't, not when she looked up at him with eyes that were glazed with desire, with want—with need.

"Yes," she said in a hoarse whisper as she tried to undo the remaining buttons on his shirt. "Yes, Rafe—*yes*."

He grabbed her hands and held them against his chest, where his heart beat beyond his control. Then he began to move into her and she began to rise against him, meeting him with her own desire, thrust for thrust.

Mine, he tried to say over and over, but his words had left him and all he could do was hold himself together until she cried out in the throes of her pleasure. When she did, when her body tightened down on him, he gave up all hope of holding himself together. He leaned forward and drove into her harder, deeper, until his climax drained him so completely that he fell forward onto her.

They lay there, breathing hard, their bodies still intertwined. Violet worked her hands free and wrapped her arms around his waist, holding him to her. "Wow, Rafe. Just…wow."

He managed to roll to one side. "A compliment, I hope?"

"Oh, yeah." She giggled again, a light sound of joy.

It made him want to laugh with her. He grinned down at her, tracing the curve of her cheek with the tip of his finger. "When we marry, it will always be like this, I think. You and I…"

His words trailed off because her mouth had twisted off to one side and her eyes had narrowed. "Violet?"

Silently, she sat up, and then stood and walked away from him. Far too late, Rafe realized what he'd said.

Married.

He had overplayed his hand.

Violet sat on the toilet, trying to figure out what had just happened. She found herself reciting the known facts.

Fact: She was pregnant.

Fact: Rafe was the father.

Fact: Sex with Rafe was, unbelievably, even better when she was stone-cold sober than when she'd been mildly buzzed.

Fact: He had just said, "When we marry."

Her brain had gotten stuck on that last word. Okay, Rafe was kind of perfect—sweet words in that liquid sunshine accent of his, hot touches that melted her. He'd even promised to look into the Wild Aces for her. Throw in the sex…

This did not mean she wanted to get married. Even if that vision of her waking up in Rafe's arms every single morning was a warm and fuzzy vision. Even if that meant raising her child—their child—together as a family. Even if…

She dropped her head in her hands, trying to get her muddled thoughts back into some semblance of order.

Not that she got far. Just back to fact number four.

When we marry. It was a statement of fact, a foregone conclusion. There was no uncertainty, no will-she-or-won't-she. Just a fact.

"Violet?"

Oh, God—the concern in Rafe's voice on the other side of the bathroom door was not making this any better.

"Are you well?" he went on.

Violet opened her mouth but closed it again when she realized she had absolutely no idea what she should say. This was all too much, too soon. A mere twenty-eight hours ago, she'd been the same woman she'd always been, one with a fond memory of their rendezvous to keep her warm on cold winter nights. There hadn't been any thought of babies and there hadn't been any thought of marriages.

She put her head between her knees. She didn't want to throw up if he was listening.

"Violet," he said in a whisper that was almost plaintive. "I did not mean…it was just…open this door, please."

"I'm—just a minute," she said, looking around. She didn't even have a robe hanging on the back of the door. Unless she wanted to wrap herself in the shower curtain, she was out of luck. She would feel much better if she could at least cover herself. "Could you go downstairs and get me a Sprite?"

"Ah…yes? Yes," he said again, sounding more sure of himself, and she had to wonder if anyone had ever asked him to fetch anything before. "I can do that for you."

"Thanks."

She exhaled when she heard the familiar creak of the floorboards as he left. Slowly, she opened her door and peeked into her room. Her clothing was scattered all over the place, but aside from that, there was no sign Rafe had been here. That's right. She'd been so turned on, she hadn't even gotten him undressed.

Okay, first things first—she got dressed. She slid her nightgown on and then pulled her light cotton robe over it. Second, she decided to go downstairs. For one thing, the odds of Rafe locating a soda on his first attempt were pretty slim. But more important, it just felt as if it'd be easier to tell him they weren't getting married anytime in the immediate future if they weren't in a bedroom that still smelled of sex.

She padded downstairs to find Rafe staring into the fridge, his eyebrows locked in a confused expression. "Ah," he said in relief when she walked in. "I can't find the Sprite."

"Here," she said, reaching around his body—of course he didn't get out of the way—and plucking the can from behind the eggs.

"Of course," he chuckled. "How did I not see that?"

"I have no idea," she said, trying to be calm.

He shut the fridge door and turned to face her. "Are you well?" he asked, resting his hand on her hip and gently drawing her toward him. His shirt was untucked but still half buttoned.

"Better," she said.

He gave her a hesitant smile, then lifted her free hand up and placed it on his heart. "Your pleasure is my pleasure," he said, pressing her fingers to his chest. "And your pain is my pain. I would never wish to upset you. And if I have done so, I regret that."

"Okay," she said, clutching the cold soda can as hard as she could because the sensation was keeping her grounded in the here and now, preventing her from being swept away by his voice and words again. "Let's get this straight, then, so there's no confusion. It's not really a good idea to tell a pregnant woman that she *will* marry you, okay?"

His eyes crinkled. "That is not done here, I take it?" Then he lifted his hand and kissed her palm again.

She smiled in spite of herself. So he'd freaked her out. But he was also capable of calming her down in a way she couldn't help but be grateful for. "Not really, no."

"Then I shall do better. But there is something between us that makes me lose my head." His eyes twinkled. "Among other things."

She could feel her concerns melting away, but she didn't want him to sweep her off her feet—again—unless things were crystal clear between them. "I don't want to get married, Rafe. I mean, I don't want to say I'll never marry you because, truthfully? You're right. There is something here. But I'm still trying to wrap my head around being pregnant. So can we just agree that we won't talk of marriage for a while?"

He pivoted and leaned back against the fridge, pulling her with him. "I understand, I really do. But you must also understand that it would bring dishonor upon my family and myself if my child were born out of wedlock."

She shouldn't be surprised by this. And honestly, she wasn't. That didn't mean it was what she wanted to hear seconds after one of the best orgasms of her life. She sagged against his chest, the soda can still in her hands. "Do we—will we have to get married? Is that what happens in your country?"

He paused. "In my family…we do not have a choice. We are married for power. Love…"

She closed her eyes. Love. They had talked about a lot of things, but love wasn't one of them.

Rafe cleared his throat. He began to rub his hands up and down her back. "It is something to consider, yes. But I have made you this promise, Violet, and I will continue to make it. I will not force you to do something you do not wish to do."

"Okay." But honestly, did she know him well enough to believe he'd keep that promise? She had no reason not to trust him. Aside from the fact that he'd used a different name when they met, everything he'd done had been up front. "Will you stay in Royal?"

"I will be here for the foreseeable future," he replied. "But I do not think I could leave Al Qunfudhah permanently. It is my home."

She nodded. "I understand."

He leaned her back and stared down into her eyes. "But I would like to suggest that we spend the time getting to know each other. Perhaps," he said gently, pressing his lips to the top of her head for a quick kiss, "it would not be such a bad thing, you and I."

"Perhaps not," she tentatively agreed.

"This is not something I can decide for you," he went on. She wanted to burrow deeper into his chest and feel his honeyed voice surround her. "You must decide that for yourself," he went on. "All I can do is show you that I will be good for you and that I will be a good father to our child."

She leaned back to look at him. "Do you always know the right thing to say?"

That made him laugh. "Based on what happened earlier, I would say the answer is no." He brushed her hair out of her face. "May I stay the night with you?"

She tried to look stern, but didn't think she was successful. "You're not going to propose marriage, are you?"

"Ah, I have many other things I would rather be doing with you," he replied, lowering his mouth to hers.

She sighed into the kiss. Everyone was always telling her what she should do, what was best. When was the last time someone had told her to make the decision?

So Rafe thought they should be married. And given the way he was devouring her, maybe they could be good together. Better than they already were.

She wasn't going to figure it out if she didn't spend some time with him, right? "Stay," she whispered against his skin.

"And tomorrow? I want to know more about you, Violet. I want to know what you do and how you live. I only have a few old stories your brother told me many years ago."

"Mac's out of town for a couple of days. If you wanted, you could ride with me tomorrow." She leaned back and looked at him. "You can ride, can't you?"

That smile—cool and confident, almost cocky. "I can. My family maintains a reputable stable of Arabians, as well as other horses. And I would love to ride with you. But I have some business to attend to in the morning," he said with a rueful smile. "You see, I have made a beautiful woman a promise that I would look into something for her and I would hate to disappoint her."

"Oh." All that languid heat flowed through her again and she thought of how good this could be. "I could meet you here after lunch? We're working calves in the morning, so all we'll have to do in the afternoon is herd the cattle to different pasture."

Something in his smile softened as he touched his fingertips to her cheek. "Mac told me you were a brilliant manager. I would love to see you in your elements, as they say."

She giggled. "In my element," she corrected and he laughed with her.

Oh, yeah, they could be good together. Usually, men said they wanted to "take her away from all this" or some such stupid claptrap, as if she only worked cattle because she had to. As if all she really wanted was to stay home, barefoot and pregnant and baking cakes. As if they could not believe that she, Violet McCallum, might actually be managing this ranch because she wanted to.

And now? Here she was with Rafe, a man who literally could take her away from all of this—away to some distant desert, as the wife of a sheikh—and what did he want? To ride with her. To see her work.

To keep his promise to her.

“Come,” he said, taking her hand and kissing it. “The morning is still a long way off.”

Six

Rafe, come on in.

Rafe smiled as he pulled the note off the front door and put it in his pocket. Then he walked into Mac McCallum's house as if he owned it.

Soon, he just might.

He had procured the services of a local Realtor, who knew Lulu Clilmer, owner of the Wild Aces. The Realtor had informed Rafe that the Wild Aces, with its 750 acres of prime grazing land, was worth approximately one million dollars but wasn't for sale at this moment in time. She even knew about Mac's leasing arrangements to access the natural springs on the Aces' land.

Rafe had instructed the woman with bouffant blond hair and too-white teeth to offer Mrs. Clilmer two million dollars cash, payable within three days.

Rafe wasn't sure the Realtor trusted him completely.

It would have been better to have a local like Nolan make the offer for Samson Oil instead of Rafe but he was not going to be deterred. And the Realtor was properly motivated by the prospect of an unexpected commission. The only snag was that she wouldn't be able to forward the offer to the owner until tomorrow because she had another closing today.

Which was fine. That gave Rafe another day or so to woo Violet. He made sure he had the box in his pocket—his other errand this morning had been to stop by a local jeweler's. Wedding Violet was almost as important as obtaining the Wild Aces.

In truth, he would prefer to have Violet's promise to wed him secured before he moved on the Wild Aces. His scheme had already undergone enough revisions recently. He did not want to further endanger it.

He stopped inside the front door and listened. Was she upstairs? That was where he had left her early this morning with a kiss and a promise to see her at noon.

Ah, humming—it was coming from the kitchen. And he smelled the scent of fried chicken.

Rafe silently padded down the hall. And there was Violet, assembling their meal. Something in his chest loosened at the sight of her. Her hair was pulled back into a low ponytail. Well-worn blue jeans hugged her hips. She was in her stocking feet and looked smaller, more delicate, than she did when she was in her boots. There was a peace around her that was almost infectious. Most any idiot could see that she was quite happy here.

A series of inexplicable urges hit him. He wanted to be the one that made her that happy. He wanted to walk up behind her and wrap his arms around her waist and kiss her neck and hold her. He wanted…he wanted things he could not put into words, but he could feel, pulling him toward her.

Last night, he had said things that he did not necessarily believe would come to pass. After he exacted his revenge, he had no plans to return to Royal, much less live here. He had told Violet he was considering those options without really meaning it. It had not been a lie—he could consider all his options without choosing to stay.

But this? Coming home at lunch to find her in the kitchen, preparing food? There was something so profoundly normal about it—normal by American standards, at least—that it made him think back to when he was still friends with her brother.

Rafe's childhood had not been one filled with carefree days and playmates. He'd been put through a rigorous education so that he would live up to the iron-fisted expectations of Hassad bin Saleed. And when he failed to meet those expectations, punishment was...harsh. Rafe had quickly learned that failure was not an option, not if he wanted to survive childhood. And although he was unable to save Fareed from any such suffering, Rafe did his best to shield his younger siblings from his father's wrath.

So when Rafe was allowed to venture out of Al Qunfudhah to America to attend Harvard, the freedom had been both sweet and somehow terrifying. It was only when Mac had befriended him that Rafe had started to understand this new world and its expectations.

And those stories... Mac had spoken so often of this house, of the people in it. How his mother still cooked dinner for them all and at least four nights a week, they were expected to sit down as a family and talk. That was such a foreign concept to Rafe. He had only dined with his father during state dinners, when he was expected to follow protocol and remain silent. To imagine a place where the mother and father openly expressed love not only for each other but also their children? Where they did things as a family?

Rafe had so desperately wanted to believe that such a world existed, that such a family existed. And he might have had a better chance to achieve that kind of harmony in his own family if he had not asked Mac to keep an eye on Nasira when she came to visit at Harvard.

In truth, Rafe had thought often of Mac's tales of his home in Royal. But he had not allowed himself to feel this unwanted nostalgia for a dream he had once nurtured and lost.

Not until now. Not until Violet.

Perhaps, if Mac had not betrayed him, this would have been Rafe's destiny. Before the incident with Nasira, they had even made plans for Rafe to make the journey to Royal, Texas, on holiday from university. Rafe would stay with Mac and meet all the people he had heard so many warm stories about—including Violet.

She would have still been in her teens. Would he have felt the beginnings of an attraction for her then? Or would she have just been Mac's irritating little sister?

He would never know. And that thought ate at him.

He slipped up behind her, slid his arms around her waist and leaned down to press his lips to the side of her neck.

"Oh!" She startled in his arms and twisted to look at him. "Rafe! I didn't hear you come in."

"I did not mean to frighten you," he said, pressing another kiss against her lips. "The meal smells delicious."

She grinned and, turning back to her preparations, leaned against him. His hands slid down and cradled her belly. "I hope fried chicken is okay," she said, lifting the chicken out and setting it on a plate to cool. On the counter were a pan of biscuits and a fresh salad.

"It will be wonderful. Here." He pulled the jeweler's box out of his pocket and opened it in front of her. "I brought you something."

She gasped as she saw the pendant. "Rafe—I didn't—I mean—*wow.*"

"This is, as I understand, an American tradition. If I have calculated correctly, our child will be born in August," he said, pointing to the light green peridot stone at the center of the pendant. "And you were born in September, correct? So the sapphire is for you."

"And the yellow?"

"Citrine for November, when I was born. It is all set in eighteen-carat white gold."

Violet touched the pendant with a tentative finger. The three stones were strung together with the sapphire first, the peridot in the middle and the citrine on the end. "It's beautiful," she exhaled. "But you really shouldn't have."

"That is nonsense," he said, removing the necklace and opening the clasp. He draped it around her neck and fastened it. "You are carrying my child, a gift I could never hope to match. This is but a small token. There." He adjusted the chain so the pendant lay against her collarbone. "It suits your beauty," he said seriously.

"Rafe," she said and he heard hesitation in her voice. "Is this—I mean, is this really happening? Do you honestly think we can make this work? Or make something work? I mean...well, I don't know what I mean. It's all happening so fast and I just don't want..." Her voice trailed off.

"I take it this was not in your plans?"

"No," she said, giving him a weak smile over her shoulder while she touched the necklace.

"Nor was any of this in my plans. But I think perhaps…" He sighed and let his hands rest against the gentle curve of her stomach again. Within grew his child. No, this was not in his plans at all. "Perhaps this was what was supposed to happen."

"Really?" She didn't bother to conceal her doubt. "You think destiny's been waiting for us to have a one-night stand, huh?"

He grinned against her neck. "Do you know that, at one point, your brother and I had made plans for me to accompany him home on break? We would have met then."

She twisted in his arms, her brow wrinkled. "I would have been, what—fifteen? Sixteen?"

"And I only twenty. Do not mistake me. I would not have made any untoward attempts on you then. I can be very patient. Of that you have no idea. I can wait years for something I want."

Odd, that. He had waited years for revenge on Mac. But what if, instead, he had merely been biding his time for this moment with Violet?

But then, what if he had come home with Mac and Violet had caught his eye twelve years ago? His father would have no sooner allowed a young Rafe to give his heart to a common American girl than he would have allowed Rafe to degrade the bin Saleed name by donning shiny pants and joining a singing group. And if Hassad bin Saleed had discovered that Rafe harbored tender feelings for Violet then, he would have had Rafe married off to the daughter of a political ally within the month and Rafe would never have had the chance to follow his own heart.

But Mac's betrayal had come first.

"I was a different person then," she said, her voice low. "My parents were still alive and I was just a kid, really."

"As was I." She dropped her gaze. He still had her in his arms, but he felt the distance between them. "What is it?"

"Rafe, what happened between you and Mac?"

He supposed that he should appreciate the fact that Violet had phrased it as a question and not an accusation. "It does not signify," he said, his jaw tight. The effort of keeping his voice light was more taxing than he might have anticipated. "What happened was a lifetime ago. I was, as you said, a different person then. It has no bearing on us at this moment."

"But..."

Rafe did the only reasonable thing he could, given the situation. He kissed Violet, hard. She stood stiffly in his arms for a moment but then relaxed into him.

"It does not signify," he repeated, tucking her against his chest. "I am not here for your brother. I am here for you. I am here for our child. Our family."

Odder still that as he said it, it did not feel like a lie.

It felt very much like the truth.

He was surprised to see her eyes fill with unshed tears. "Are you unwell?" he asked hurriedly.

"I'm fine," she said, giving him a watery smile and dabbing at her eyes with the cuff of her sleeve. "It's just the hormones. Okay. Whoo." She exhaled heavily and put on a brighter smile for him. "There."

He was not entirely convinced. "I can still have a private doctor here inside of twenty-four hours."

She waved this suggestion away. "I'm fine," she repeated. "It's just that you have no idea how refreshing it is to know that you don't care about going through my brother."

Ah, yes. His scheme. The one that now hinged on convincing this woman that she wanted to spend the rest of her life with him so that she would turn her back on Mac. He wanted to be impressed that it was going so smoothly, but as she blotted at another stray tear, that was not the emotion that welled in his chest.

"In my country, it is customary to ask permission of a woman's father before you court her," he told her. "Or, if her father is not available, her oldest living male relative."

Violet held her breath. "Oh? You're not going to do that now, are you? I haven't even told Mac about my pregnancy or anything."

"No," he assured her, wrapping his arms around her again and pulling her against his chest. "You forget something."

"What's that?"

"We are not in my country."

Her head lifted and this time, her smile was not forced. "We're not, are we?"

"Not even close. So," he said, cupping her cheek in his hand. "Let us eat this delicious meal and then you can show me what you do. For our child will be a bin Saleed and there are expectations that go along with that, but that child will also be a McCallum and it would be best if they knew how to manage a ranch, would it not?"

Her expression should not make him feel this, well, *good*. Nothing about her except for the sex should make him feel this good. But everything about her did. "It would. And tonight? Will you stay again?"

"I will not leave your side until you tell me to go."

"Good," she said. "Then I want you to stay."

Watching Rafe mount Two Bit was a thing of beauty and quite possibly a joy forever. Good heavens, that man in a pair of blue jeans was the stuff of dreams, Violet decided. She wouldn't have guessed that Rafe could so easily slip into the role of a cowboy but, appearance-wise, he was doing just that. The jeans and the button-down shirt with mother-of-pearl buttons looked completely natural on his athletic form. Hell, he even pulled the hat off with plenty of grit to spare.

Who would have guessed that her sheikh was hiding a cowboy underneath those dark eyes and smoldering gazes? It was hard to disguise the imperial lift of his chin, though.

"Two Bit," he said as he got his seat in the Western saddle. He took up the reins in two hands, but caught himself and switched both to one hand. "That is a quarter of a dollar, correct?"

"Yup. But he's also a quarter horse. All my cutting horses are," Violet said, swinging up onto Skipper's back. Rafe's eyes got wide. "Oh, come on. I'm only a little bit pregnant. Skipper's a good old mare and I've been riding her for years. Trust me, there's nothing dangerous about this. In three or four months, maybe. But I have no plans to ride hell-for-leather today."

"All right," he said doubtfully. "Where are we going?"

"We've been working calves," she explained, gathering Skipper's reins and heading toward the northwest pasture. "We castrate them, brand them and vaccinate them all at one time. But we do that in the morning, when the sun's low and it's still cool. Puts less stress on the animal. So now, we're going to move the calves and the cows from the pasture where we worked them this morning to a different pasture and then round up another group and shuffle them in so they'll be ready to be worked tomorrow morning."

As she talked, she kept a close eye on Rafe's face.

What would he think of her after *that* little lecture? Because thus far, he'd mostly only seen her in dresses at hotels and restaurants. But that wasn't who she really was.

This—crap on her boots, wearing blue jeans and half chaps that covered her thighs—this was who she was.

Could he handle it? Or would his vision of his beautiful, mysterious V be destroyed by a whole lot of cows?

"I gather that being a ranch manager is a hands-on job," he said without wincing at the word *castrate*.

Which was impressive. Most of the men around here—men who castrated plenty of calves on their own—got a look of dread on their faces when Violet said the word out loud.

"It is," she agreed.

"What will you do when you are no longer able to—what is the phrase? Saddle up and ride?"

She shot him a smile. "Good! I've got a good crew. I'll have to hire a few more hands and my crew leader, Dale, will have to take on a bit more responsibility." It wasn't going to be easy to back away from her position like that, but at a certain point when her belly just got too big, she was going to have to accept reality. "We have a Gator, a minitruck I can use to get out into the pastures."

"And when the baby comes?" His tone was not judgmental, nor was he issuing any sort of edicts. Thank heavens for that.

She laughed, but she didn't miss the way it sounded nervous to her own ears. "I'm still working on that. I've only been aware of this pregnancy for a couple of days."

"Ah, yes. I am sorry. One day at a time, correct?"

"Correct."

He was silent for a while and they rode on. Violet pointed out land features as they went. "That's our spring and over there? Those empty concrete pads? That's where our water tanks were," she said. "The tornado ripped our tanks right off their moorings like they were empty pop cans."

"But you could have replaced the tanks, yes?"

"We did. But the spring got messed up. We're not sure what happened—before the tornado, the spring was fine and we had water reserves in abundance. But after the tornado, the cows refused to drink the water and our reserves were gone. Mac thought maybe some fracking that had been happening to our east had something to do with it, but we're not sure."

"But you have water now, correct?"

"Yup. Our tanks are now up on the property line dividing the Double M and the Wild Aces. The Aces has a bunch of springs, including one not that far from the property line. It's the only reason Mac agreed to leasing the Wild Aces—for the water."

Rafe thought this over for a while. "Why did he not allow you to buy the land? You obviously want it."

Violet sighed so heavily that Skipper's ears swiveled back. She leaned forward to pat the horse's neck in reassurance. "I don't know." Rafe turned in his saddle to give her a look. "No, really, I don't. I don't know if he thinks I'm incapable of being on my own or if he just feels more in control of the world if I'm under the same roof. He wasn't here when our parents died and I'm not sure he's ever forgiven himself for it."

"So he did not make a wise business decision because…something might happen to you?" Rafe sounded genuinely confused by this.

"As best I can guess." Rafe was staring at her as if he understood the words, but the meaning was lost on him. "What? Didn't your family try to protect you?"

"Ah," Rafe said in a way that Violet was pretty sure

meant no. "I believe the whole reason my father had children—aside from Fareed, who is the ruler—was to use them to make 'wise business decisions,' as you have said."

Use? Had he really just said *use* like that, like it was this common thing? Sure, her parents expected her and Mac to do their fair share of chores around the ranch, starting when she was three and had the job of making sure the horses' water buckets in the barn were full, but that wasn't the same kind of expectation as being used for business-related purposes. "Really? Didn't your parents love you?"

"My mother, I am sure, felt affection toward us."

Now it was Violet's turn to stare. "'Felt affection'? Didn't she ever tell you she loved you?"

Rafe was silent for far too long and she wasn't sure if the conversation was over or not. Maybe this cultural divide was bigger than she'd thought?

But then Rafe said, "Love is a weakness and weaknesses can be used against you," in such a way that a chill ran down her spine.

"That sounds…awful."

"It was quite normal for us. It is not until you get out into the world and see how other people live that you begin to question your upbringing."

"I never got out into the world," she said quietly. "I've never left home."

"But you will. You will always have a place in Al Qunfudhah as the mother of a royal child."

Another shudder ran through her. Was this what awaited her in this far-off desert country? A royal life with a man who had been raised to believe that showing love—or even affection—to a baby was a weakness?

But how did that mesh with the man who whispered

sweet words in that liquid-honey voice of his, who brought her an expensive necklace symbolizing their birthdays and the future birthday of their baby? A man who had promised he'd look into the Wild Aces for her?

Was that love?

Or was it a wise business decision?

"It was not until I went to Harvard that I saw things could be different," Rafe went on, missing her stunned silence. "I was quite unsure how to understand your brother's closeness to his family, to you."

And then there was that—that unspoken event involving Rafe, his sister and Mac that had destroyed the two men's friendship. Earlier in the kitchen, Rafe had spoken of that time as if it were his fondest memory. It was obvious that Rafe had considered Mac a brother then.

But there were other instances when the mention of Mac's name brought a hard edge to Rafe's eyes—a hardness that Violet couldn't overlook. And she had to wonder what, exactly, Rafe thought of her brother now.

"Were you close to your brothers and sisters growing up?" she asked in a careful tone.

"I did try to protect the younger ones." He gave her a rueful smile. "On that, your brother and I agreed." He turned his gaze away. "To a point."

"And you're not going to tell me what happened? Does it somehow not 'signify'?"

Rafe attempted a careless shrug but, unlike the hat and boots, he couldn't pull it off. She got the feeling that *careless* wasn't in his vocabulary. "In the end, it was for the best. Nasira was promised to a warlord much older than she and, once she was ruined, the warlord released her from her obligations. After that, my father no longer cared what she did, so she was able to leave Al Qunfudhah and marry a man more to her liking."

Ruined. That was, hands down, the ugliest word Violet had ever heard. And Rafe had said it so easily, as if he now thought less of his sister for what she'd done with Mac.

Was that it? Mac and Nasira had taken a liking to each other and Rafe disapproved because he believed Mac had ruined his sister?

Doubt flickered through her mind. This thing with Rafe was happening so fast—was the attraction between them real or was there something else going on here?

"I'm happy for her," she managed to get out in a tight voice. "I'd love to meet her sometime."

"I shall arrange it. But I do not know if she will come to Texas. She resides in England with her husband. They are quite happy, I believe."

They were silent for a bit longer as they approached the pasture where her cows and calves were anxious to begin the trip back out to the wide-open spaces. "Would it be possible to ride out to this other ranch, the Wild Aces, after we are done here? I would love for you to show it to me."

"Yeah."

Rafe looked out over the spring Texas landscape and sighed. There was something in his face—something that looked more relaxed than she'd seen him yet. "It is your dream, is it not?"

"It is." Violet nudged Skipper into a trot. "So let's get moving."

Seven

Violet's workers greeted her warmly and they all tipped their hats to Rafe. No one questioned her statement that Rafe was an old friend of Mac's visiting. And, Rafe noted, no one questioned her skills.

One of the workers swung open a gate and the calves came hurrying out. Rafe watched with interest as the larger cows and smaller calves all paired off. The noise was something new to him. They did not exactly have herds of cattle wandering around Al Qunfudhah. Camels, yes. Arabian horses, yes. Cattle? No.

"Rafe," Violet called. "To your left—we've got a straggler!"

Rafe twisted in his saddle and saw a cow leaving the group as it was herded north. The animal was moving at a good pace and the distance between it and the rest of the cows was quickly growing.

"What should I do?" he called back. He did not miss

the way several of the cowboys laughed under their breath at him.

Embarrassment burned at his ears, but he kept his attention on Violet. "Try to get in front of the cow," she called back. "I'll be right there."

Rafe touched his heels to the horse's side. He may not know the best way to retrieve a wayward cow, but he would be damned if he allowed this beast to outrun him on horseback.

Two Bit leaped into a flat-out run. Rafe held the reins awkwardly in one hand, but the horse responded to his heels wonderfully. Rafe gave the animal his head and trusted his footing.

Behind him, he heard a loud whoop, but he did not know if it was Violet or one of the men who had laughed at him.

Rafe smiled as he leaned over Two Bit's neck. The wind ripped his hat from his head, but he didn't give it a moment's thought.

Oh, how he loved to ride. His father had kept a stable of prizewinning Arabian horses and expected his children to ride and ride well. Anything less than expert horsemanship would have brought shame upon the bin Saleed house.

Rafe's daily rides were the time of his greatest joys, for then, he was free.

Just as he felt free now. The wind ripped at his clothes as he urged Two Bit to go faster. They shot past the stray cow and then, using only his knees, Rafe got Two Bit turned back. The horse stopped and spun, startling the cow to such a degree that the animal froze.

They all stood there, Rafe and Two Bit and the cow, as if none of them were sure what to do next. He had done as Violet had told him—he had gotten ahead of the cow and the animal had stopped. But now what?

Out of nowhere, a looped rope sailed through the air and landed around the neck of the cow. "Gotcha," Violet said, trotting up.

"You roped that cow in one shot? I am impressed," Rafe said, watching as Violet tied the other end of the rope around the horn of her Western saddle and began to pull the stubborn cow back to the herd.

She shot him a smile. "Get up, Bossy," she snapped at the cow, who reluctantly began to move.

When the cow was safely back with its brethren and she had removed her rope, one of the other cowboys rode up to Rafe and said, "Oowee, man—that was some fancy riding! Didn't expect that from a city slicker—no offense."

He looked at the man with a bemused smile. "None taken. I normally ride Arabians, but this is quite a mount." He leaned forward and patted the horse's neck as he glanced at Violet. "I believe Two Bit is worth far more than twenty-five cents."

Everyone laughed at that—but this time, they weren't laughing at Rafe. And he once again had that out-of-time experience where this whole thing could have easily happened twelve years ago, except with Mac by his side instead of Violet.

He was glad, however, that it was Violet by his side now.

"I trained him myself," Violet said as they spread out along the vast herd of cattle to keep any more from wandering off.

"He rode beautifully. I have not spent much time on other horses besides my own—but it was wonderful."

"Cowboy," Violet said, giving him a look that heated

his blood, "any time you want to come back and ride hell for leather, you just let me know."

It was some hours later, with the sun already setting, when Violet said farewell to her workers. The cowboys all departed, but Violet and Rafe stayed out in the pastures on horseback, riding farther away from the Double M.

"You are quite good at this," Rafe said. They were speaking softly. With dusk closing in around them, the sky lighting up in golds and reds like a tapestry woven of the finest silk, Rafe felt as if the world had been made just for them.

"You say that like you're surprised," she teased, a wide smile on her face.

"I would not have guessed that my mysterious, beautiful V could rope and ride half so good as you do."

"Does this mean you're going to stop worrying about me riding a horse?"

"I shall certainly worry less," he promised. "But no, I do not think I can stop worrying about you."

She seemed to consider this. "Will you be able to come to the appointment with me? It's in twelve days. I think I'll be able to hear a heartbeat."

"I would not miss such a chance. But," he added as they began to climb a low rise, "we must consider beyond that."

Even in the rosy evening light, he saw the color drain from her face. "I don't even know where to begin. Can we wait? Until after the appointment? I just feel like if I have a doctor's seal of approval and everything's okay, it'll be easier to decide what to do next."

"We can wait," he promised her. It was a sincere promise because Rafe had no desire to upset her. But it also played into his scheme nicely. The longer Violet withheld this secret from Mac, the more the betrayal would sting when Violet accompanied Rafe to Al Qunfudhah.

But as soon as he had that thought, a sense of discomfort overtook Rafe. After spending the afternoon working and riding with Violet on her well-trained horses, he was having a great deal of difficulty picturing her ensconced in his royal home in Al Qunfudhah, with miles of sand surrounding her instead of a sea of waving grass. She seemed as much a part of this land as the grass and sky. It felt wrong, somehow, to take her away from her home. It would be like caging a wild horse and breaking its spirit.

Could he really do that to her? It went against his every urge to protect her and their child.

What muddled his thinking was that she genuinely appeared to care for him in a way that no one else ever had. What if he never found another woman who felt this way about him? What if, by breaking Violet's spirit, he destroyed his last—his only—chance for happiness?

He shook those thoughts from his head. He was not destined for happiness. The past few days with Violet had been nothing but a…a diversion. A pleasant one, to be sure, but a diversion nonetheless. The only wrong he had to concern himself with here was avenging the wrongs done to his family honor. That was all that mattered.

"Here," she said, breaking him out of his reverie as they crested the hill. She reined her mount to a halt. "That," she said, sweeping her hand out over the vista before them, "is the Wild Aces."

Rafe had, of course, seen a few pictures of it. But the beauty of the land, bathed in the glow of the sunset, took his breath away. He could see how the land differed from the Double M—the trees were larger and more grouped and the grasses were a deeper green, especially around the springs that dotted the land. "It is lovely," he said.

"Down there," she said, pointing south, "those are our tanks. And then there? To the north? That's the house."

Rafe looked in the direction she was pointing and saw a grand old home standing in a grove of tall trees. Clusters of yellow rosebushes crowded around the building's foundation; even at this distance, Rafe could see the blooms. A long drive led away from the house and that, too, had trees planted along it. The home seemed as much a part of the land as everything else.

"I love this place," Violet said with a satisfied sigh. "The house needs to be updated, though. Lulu—that's the current owner—has lived there for close to forty years and she's getting on in age. Renovations haven't exactly been on her radar. Plus, she smokes—a lot—so I'd want the whole house cleaned inside and out before I raise a kid there."

A twinge of an unfamiliar emotion took hold of Rafe so suddenly that he had to rub at a spot in his chest that began physically aching. He needed the Wild Aces to complete his revenge on Mac but…

It would not just hurt Mac, what he was doing. It would hurt Violet, too.

Nonsense, he tried to tell himself. First off, Violet would be joining him in Al Qunfudhah—that was the plan, and he would not allow his sentimental feelings for her to change that plan.

The necklace had merely been the first of such gifts. The day after tomorrow, he would bring her a bracelet of diamonds and rubies and then, a ring—diamond, as required by American tradition. If he were still at home, he would not wait a day to bring her jewels, but Violet had shown enough hesitation over their plan that Rafe did not want to rush her too much. More than he had to, anyway.

And besides, once Rafe had the Wild Aces and had broken Mac, well—Rafe would still have the Wild Aces. And he would also have the Double M. There was nothing that prevented him from keeping the land for Violet, just so long as Mac did not benefit from the arrangement.

This realization made the pain in his chest ease. One way or the other, the Wild Aces would be Violet's. Then she would no longer have to rely on her brother's permission to do anything.

"It will be perfect," he told her in all sincerity. And it would be.

All it required was a little more patience.

Patience was, at this exact moment, something Rafe had in perilously short supply. The last thing he wanted to be doing right now was attending some meeting at some club under false pretenses of perhaps joining the club at some point in the undefined future. He had no intention of settling down in Royal, Texas.

Or at least, he hadn't until two days ago.

He wanted to be back with Violet, and the strength of this feeling was worrisome. He had spent two nights in Violet's arms, in her bed—sharing her body and her dreams. That he had been forced to give that up only because Mac returned from his business trip did not improve Rafe's mood.

Violet was pregnant with *his* child. He felt reasonably certain of that, as certain as a man could feel without blood tests. She had agreed that, at the doctor's appointment, they would get the test that confirmed what they already knew—for Fareed and for Mac.

It bothered Rafe that they both needed to operate in

such a manner to prove to their older brothers beyond a shadow of a doubt that the child was theirs. Rafe had vowed to never again be in a position where Mac held sway over him, and yet now Rafe was sitting next to Mac, pretending as if this situation did not bother him in the least.

The Realtor had been in contact today. She would be making an offer on the Wild Aces in the morning. It was the last piece of the puzzle Rafe had been slowly assembling over the past six months, and he was eager to have it in place.

Violet wanted the ranch not only for land or water but because that was where she wanted to make her home. That was where she wanted to raise their child.

With him?

He was still unclear on that. He had foolhardily mentioned marriage while his head had still been clouded with passion on their second night together—and what a mistake that had been. For a man who was actively trying to convince her to choose him over her brother, it was clear that telling Violet what to do would always be a mistake.

No, if he wanted Violet to abandon Mac, he had to convince her that was what she wanted. And to do that…

Rafe had not often awoken with a woman in his arms. But that was exactly the position he had found himself in the previous two mornings when sleep had left him. He had been on his back and Violet had been curled on her side against him.

It should have felt wrong. Or odd, at the very least. But with Violet exhaling her warm breath against his chest, her breasts pressed against his side, Rafe had felt an unexpected calm. It was almost as if she belonged there.

That feeling had only gotten stronger as he had awoken her with a kiss. With more than one kiss, in fact. He had lost count.

It felt as if a sandstorm had been unleashed upon him and he had no way to protect himself. The facts as he knew them spun faster and faster around his mind until he was dizzy and raw.

"...Started admitting women a couple of years ago," Mac was saying as they drove toward the dim lights of Royal. "It's not the same club my father joined, but I don't have a problem with that."

"Is Violet a member?" Rafe asked. What he needed right now was additional information. He wanted to be absolutely certain that Violet was exactly as she said she was. He could not bear the thought that somehow, the McCallum siblings were working together against him.

The trick was to extract the information without arousing Mac's suspicions. It was possible, however. One of the more applicable lessons his father had taught him was to keep your friends close and your enemies closer. And if your enemy still thought of himself as a friend, well, it made things that much easier.

Right now, all Rafe knew of Violet was a collection of disparate facts that did not necessarily add up. Violet was Mac's baby sister, the one he had worried about, the young girl who'd gotten into all sorts of scrapes and hijinks, forever driving their parents to distraction.

She was a cowgirl who trained horses for cutting and roped cattle and pined for a place of her own.

But Violet was also his V, beautiful and passionate, the rare woman who had made Rafe break his long stretch of celibacy. She was the woman who had haunted the edge of his dreams for months now. The woman who had made him consider breaking his promise of one night, no strings, and having Nolan, his lawyer, look into finding her.

And she was the woman, soft and tousled with sleep but still capable of bringing him the greatest of pleasure, who had cried out his name in the morning. She was the woman whose rounded belly contained his child growing within.

The thought of Nolan was a source of pain and Rafe welcomed it. Anything to break his thoughts from Violet. He had come so far, he could not let this…this infatuation with her destroy his scheme.

Nolan had been his friend, his trusted second here in America as Rafe set the wheels of his plan into motion. But Nolan had turned on Rafe just as Mac had all those years ago—Nolan had found a woman and decided that love was more important.

Not that what Mac and Nasira had had was love. Even Rafe understood how lust could drive a man to do things far outside his normal character. But Nasira…

Rafe struggled to remember what his sister had said to him at the time, in hidden whispers on the long trip back to Al Qunfudhah. She had not wanted to marry the man their father had chosen for her—a much older man, a tribal warlord with a reputation for cruelty who had children nearly as old as Nasira herself. She had not wanted to be forced into a marriage. She had wanted to choose. And she was sorry—deeply sorry—that Rafe had been hurt, but his friend had been a better choice than the warlord.

Which brought Rafe's whirling sandstorm of thoughts right back to Violet. Was what she wanted so very different from what Nasira had gone to great lengths to get? The right to choose her husband?

This thought troubled him. It troubled him greatly.

"She hasn't really been interested in joining," Mac was saying. "And truthfully, I haven't really encouraged her. I know what some of those guys are like. They're fine for kicking back and having a beer with in the evening, but I don't want them around my baby sister. They're not good enough for her, you know?"

"You are very protective of her," Rafe said.

"I just don't want anything bad to happen to her, you know? After our parents…" Mac cleared his throat.

Rafe would not allow himself to think fondly of Violet. He would absolutely not allow his baser instincts to override everything else. Instead, he would focus on his reason for being here—avenging his family honor. Nasira. Oh, yes. Rafe was going to make this man pay and pay dearly. How could he sit there and wax poetic about protecting his own flesh and blood after having so callously used Rafe's sister?

"So she does not date among the men from your club?" Mac looked at him sideways and Rafe knew he was treading on dangerous ground. "You did ask me to keep an eye on her. If she is dating someone of whom you approve, I would not want to interfere in that relationship. That is not how things work in my country."

He let the words "in my country" hang in the air. Once, he had tried to explain his culture in general and his family structure in particular to his American friends but it was more difficult than bridging the language divide.

Compared to many other Middle Eastern countries, Al Qunfudhah had an extremely liberal view of women's rights. Women could drive and hold jobs and they had the right to refuse a suitor—well, commoners did, anyway. That had not been true of Nasira or any of the sheikh's children—at least, not under Hassad bin Saleed. His brother Fareed was changing those rules, as well.

But the cultural requirement that a man ask permission of a woman's father or brother before a date in all circumstances did not sit well with most Americans. Perhaps that was one of the reasons Rafe and Mac had been such good friends so quickly—Mac, better than anyone else Rafe had met at Harvard, had understood the impulse to protect sisters.

If Mac believed that Rafe's questions were about Mac's approval or disapproval of his sister's dating, not an effort to ascertain whether or not she engaged with many gentlemen friends, well, that only made Rafe look better. He was supporting his friend's right to rule his family as he saw fit.

"No, no—she doesn't date much. I haven't met the man worthy of her, frankly, and I don't want her wasting her time on losers who are only after one thing."

Well. That certainly lent credence to Violet's claim that in the last year she had only been with Rafe.

This what she was hiding from, the night they spent together. Rafe remembered asking why she was just V—was it family or lovers? And she had not answered the question.

He knew now. She was hiding from family. From the very man Rafe was honor bound to destroy.

This certainly put an interesting twist on things.

Rafe never would have guessed when he made this trip to America that he would be eager to attend a doctor's appointment. His father had never stooped so low as to concern himself with the health of the mother of his children. But Rafe was not his father, thank heavens.

Eleven more days until the appointment, where he

hoped to hear his child's heartbeat, felt a very long time off.

"Here we are," Mac said, pulling up outside a long, low building with immaculate landscaping. "The Texas Cattleman's Club—it missed the worst of the tornado we had last year."

"Mac!" Rafe spun to see a cowboy waving at Mac through the open doors of the clubhouse. "Good to see you, man."

"Hey, Chance. Chance, this is an old friend of mine, Rafe bin Saleed. Rafe, Chance McDaniel."

Rafe shook hands and the two men talked about Chance's new daughter. Rafe looked at pictures of a small, wrinkly baby with rather more interest than he might have otherwise. Was this in his future, a baby like this? "What age?" he asked Chance. He had no experience with babies or even children, for that matter. When his siblings had been younger, they had had nannies and nurses and Rafe had only seen them briefly in the evening, when all the children were brought together and presented for their father's inspection.

"Four months. God, Gabriella's just a natural. I didn't think I could love her more," he said, his gaze fastened on the next picture, which was of a beautiful dark-haired woman holding the baby, who was now wearing a frilly pink dress. "You have any kids, Rafe?"

"Ah, no." He swallowed, uncharacteristically nervous. Until several days ago, there had been no possibility of him having children.

Chance snorted in a good-natured way. "They change everything, kids." He clapped Mac on the back. "I keep telling this guy to settle down, but he's too busy!"

For the first time, the possibility of being a father—outside of wedlock, no less—hit Rafe as a real thing and not just a countermove in his scheme. What would his family think if they found out that Rafe had impregnated Violet? He honestly did not know. His father would have done horrible things in the name of the family honor. Being forced to marry Violet would have been a blessing, compared to what Hassad bin Saleed might have done. But Fareed was a different man and a different ruler.

Still, if Rafe did not marry Violet, he would bring dishonor onto the family, and Fareed would not let that stand.

"Rafe here's thinking about relocating to Royal," Mac said after they had looked at the many pictures of the little girl. "I invited him to a meeting—if he buys some land, he'd be a good member."

"Great," Chance said. Rafe noticed that other men and a few women were all moving back into a larger room. "Oh, shoot—we're late. Come on."

They joined the rest of the group. Mac introduced Rafe around and Rafe shook many hands. Normally, he would be collecting information on each member, examining their connections to Mac. He did recognize several names as people from whom his front corporation, Samson Oil, had purchased land.

But he had trouble focusing because his mind kept returning back to the questions he had yet to answer.

"Case Baxter," a man said, giving Rafe's hand a vigorous shake. "I'll be running the meeting tonight, so if you have any questions, just let me know, okay?"

Rafe nodded and made polite noises of agreement, but his thoughts turned right back to Violet. How could he get her to leave this place with him without breaking her spirit? That was quite a problem—one for which he did not yet have an answer.

"This is my friend Rafiq bin Saleed, a sheikh from

Al Qunfudhah," Mac said to the group. Rafe snapped to attention at the mention of his name. "He's looking to get into the energy business and he might relocate here to Royal. I think it'd be great if we could welcome him into the club!"

There were murmurs, some of approval and some of disapproval. Rafe remembered his American manners and nodded and smiled as warmly as he could while the sandstorm of his mind continued to whirl around winning Violet McCallum.

That would be the ultimate revenge, would it not? First Rafe would destroy Mac's beloved ranch and then his beloved town and then Rafe would marry Mac's beloved sister and whisk her away to Al Qunfudhah, where…

Where Rafe would take her to bed every night. Where her pleasure would be his pleasure.

A voice cut through his reverie. "Rafiq, huh?"

Rafe turned to see a man he did not know standing near the front of the room. His arms were crossed and he looked defensive. More than defensive—he looked dangerous.

This was a challenge, and challenges had to be met head-on. Rafe stood. In times like this, his first instinct was always to do as his father had taught him—rule by force. But Americans were a different breed and Rafe had learned it was best to come at them from the side. "My friends call me Rafe," he said in the congenial tone that worked best with Americans. "And you are?"

"Kyle Wade," the man said stiffly. "Why don't you tell them who you really are?"

Rafe froze. That was the kind of statement that started off badly and only got worse.

Mac interceded on his behalf. "Hey, Kyle—I've

known Rafe since college. We're old friends. He is who he says he is, so maybe ease off a bit on my guest?"

Kyle didn't ease off. Instead, eyes narrowed, he said, "Oh? So you know that Rafiq bin Saleed is the man behind Samson Oil—the company that has been buying up land all around town?" A collective gasp went up from the other members. "Care to explain yourself there, Rafiq? Why have you been buying up property for months?"

Rafe was not the kind of man who panicked. Panicking was a waste of energy that was better spent fixing a situation. Years of enduring Hassad's rages had schooled him well in keeping his features calm and his breathing regular. He resolved to be like the stone that felt nothing.

But if he were capable of panic, he might be feeling it right now. Because suddenly, one huge part of his scheme had exploded in his face, and the feeling of being sucked into a swirling sandstorm was that much stronger. If he were not careful, he would be buried up to his neck in his own lies.

Mac turned to him, confusion and suspicion on his face. At least at the moment, the confusion was winning. "Rafe? Is that true?"

No, he was not panicking. He was a bin Saleed. If anything, he was furious at this Kyle Wade for potentially undermining his plan. Kyle would soon learn not to cross him.

He would, however, prefer not to have any more disruptions to his scheme *today.*

He waved his hand in dismissal and made an effort to look casual. The key to escaping this situation with the bulk of his scheme intact was to play up the cultural differences. "As I said, I'm looking to get into the energy business. Is this not how it is done in this country? Do you not buy land for the exploration of mineral rights?"

"None of that land has any oil left on it," shouted a man from the back of the room. "Why do you think we sold it to Samson Oil? Only a fool would think they're going to strike oil on property we've tapped out!"

Rafe gritted his teeth. He was no fool, and to imply it was to risk his wrath. This was why he had not revealed himself to Mac and the town earlier. Too late, he saw that he should have remained in the shadows until his plans were complete, until he had the Wild Aces and Mac's water had been cut off completely.

In that respect, the man was right—Rafe was a fool who had shown his hand too soon. It would be his last mistake, that was for certain.

But then Mac put his hand on Rafe's shoulder. Odd, really, how that vestigial touch of friendship could still be reassuring. "Listen," Mac said loudly over the growing buzz of people talking. "I vouch for Rafe. They do things differently in Al Qunfudhah, where he's from. If he says he's exploring mineral rights, then..." Mac looked at him and despite this very public declaration of support, Rafe could see the distrust in Mac's eyes. But then a harder expression came over his face and he turned back to the crowd. "Then I believe him," he finished.

Ah, this was excellent. Mac truly had no idea that Rafe was here to destroy him. And the fact that Mac was using his influence to convince other people that Rafe was no danger to them only made the revenge that much sweeter because when Rafe destroyed Mac, the whole town would blame Mac for vouching for his "old friend."

Rafe put his best effort into smiling warmly and shaking Mac's hand and looking as innocent as possible.

Which must have been innocent enough because Case

Baxter called the meeting back to order and everyone sat down. While the group discussed club business, Rafe mentally rearranged his plans. Above all else, Rafe had to close the deal on the Wild Aces as soon as possible. The Double M could not survive without the water from the Wild Aces. And if Rafe had a moment of doubt, a moment when he felt guilty about Violet wanting to raise their child on the Wild Aces…

No such doubt existed, and if it did, Rafe pushed it away. Caring for Violet was a weakness and at this late stage, it was a weakness he could not afford.

He had much work to do.

Eight

Violet's phone buzzed. Of course it did. She was in the middle of branding and castrating calves, for God's sake. It was messy work that required her full concentration and she was glad for that because it had been two days since Rafe had slipped out of her bed at six in the morning and kissed her goodbye with a promise that he would see her very soon.

Apparently, very soon meant something different in Al Qunfudhah than it did here in Texas, because there'd been radio silence for the past forty-eight hours and she was starting to get twitchy.

"Here," she said to Dale, her hired hand. "Hold this calf. I've got to take this call." She managed to get loose of the animal without getting kicked.

Hopefully, this was Rafe. No, she didn't really expect another rose or a love note—not when they'd both agreed that they were going to keep their previous acquaintance quiet for the time being, just until they got things settled a little more.

But again—days of radio silence? The only reason she knew that Rafe hadn't skipped town was that he'd gone to that Texas Cattleman's Club meeting with Mac the night before last.

She got out of earshot from her hired hands and pulled out her phone. It wasn't Rafe, dammit. It was, however, Lulu Clilmer, the current owner of the Wild Aces. "Hello?"

"Violet, honey," Lulu began in her gravelly, two-packs-a-day-for-forty-years voice, "I wanted to call you personally."

"Hey, Lulu, what's up? Are you all right? Do you need me to come over?" For years now, Violet had been helping Lulu out, partly because it was the neighborly thing to do but also because Violet wanted the Wild Aces, dang it all.

"I'm fine, honey. Listen, I know that you've always had your heart set on this place..."

Violet smiled nervously—which was pointless, as Lulu wouldn't have been able to video call anyone if her life depended on it. "Yeah. I've been trying to convince Mac to buy you out, but you know how he is."

"Well, honey—I don't know how to say this but..." Violet held her breath. "I've had an offer."

Violet's breath caught in her throat. Was that what Rafe had been doing? Had he spent the past two days "looking into" the Wild Aces for her? For their family? "Oh?" Violet said, not even bothering to sound cool or calm about it. "Who? Anyone I know?" *Please say Rafe. Please.*

Because if it were Rafe, then—finally—the Wild Aces would be hers. She wouldn't have to go through her brother any longer. God, she could hardly wait.

But if it wasn't Rafe...well, if it were someone else, she'd just have to push Mac harder or head down to the bank and see how much of a counteroffer she could scrape together. She was half owner of the Double M, after all. All that land equity had to count for something, right?

"Naw, honey—I'm sorry. It's some outfit that goes by the name Samson Oil."

Violet's heart plummeted down to around her knees.

"I never heard of them before—they're not local, that's for sure," Lulu continued. If it'd been someone local, there was always the chance Violet could reason with the other buyer. But some out-of-towner?

Wait—Rafe wasn't local. "Did you talk with Rafiq bin Saleed? Is he connected with Samson Oil?" She dug deep, hoping that something might ring a bell with Lulu. "Or someone named Ben, maybe?"

"Honey, no. I had been waiting on you, you know—I was happy to lease the land to you in the meantime—but the money this Samson Oil is offering? I can't walk away from this offer. I'm too old to keep this place up and my medical bills..." She trailed off into coughing.

Oh, God. This was, quite possibly, the worst-case scenario. "How much?" she asked weakly, covering her stomach with her hand as a wave of nausea appeared out of nowhere. She was just getting used to the idea of being a mother to Rafe's child. How much more disruption could she take?

There was a pause, which was followed by Lulu coughing some more. "Two," she said when she finally had her voice back.

"Million?" But Violet didn't have to ask. She already knew.

The Wild Aces was worth close to one million dollars.

Lulu had been willing to let Violet have it for $800,000, but Mac had thought that much money for that amount of land was a waste of resources. Lulu had promised that she wouldn't consider selling the Wild Aces out from under Violet for anything less than $1.5 million.

"I sure am sorry, honey," Lulu said again.

Violet put a hand to her head, as if that could get it to stop spinning. It didn't. "What if—what if I come up with a counteroffer?"

"Sweetie, we both know you don't have that much money lying around," Lulu said sympathetically.

She didn't—but McCallum Enterprises did. The company had plenty of capital. "Can you just hold off for a couple of days? Just give me the chance to make a counteroffer, okay?"

There was another long pause; Violet didn't know if Lulu was having trouble breathing again or if she was going to say no. "This Samson Oil—they want the deal done as soon as possible," Lulu said sadly.

"Just two days. A day, even," Violet pleaded. "Let me talk to Mac one more time. If I can get you $1.5 million, would you consider selling the Wild Aces to me?"

Lulu sighed heavily. "Sure thing, honey. I'll give you twenty-four hours."

Violet knew that it was only because she'd spent the past several years helping Lulu out around the house that the older woman was throwing her that small bone. "Thanks, Lulu. I'll be in touch, I promise." She ended the call and stood there, staring at her phone.

Samson Oil? Who—or what—the hell was that? No—wait. It sounded familiar. Hadn't she heard something about Samson Oil buying up a bunch of land around Royal for the oil rights? She remembered people talking about it at the Royal Diner when she'd gone in for coffee one morning a couple of months ago. Some folks had been suspicious, but others had been laughing because some dumb corporation was snapping up nearly worthless land at insane prices.

Like offering Lulu twice what the Wild Aces was worth—that was insane. This whole situation was insane. When had her nice, quiet life gotten so completely out of control? It was as if Violet's reality had been stripped away from her and she'd been thrust into some alternative universe where up was down, left was right and she was living out a soap-opera plot. She looked around, but didn't see J. R. Ewing and his big hat anywhere.

Suddenly, Violet was mad. At her brother, at Rafe, at this Samson Oil—at the universe. What the hell had she done to deserve this? Okay, yes, the one-night stand with Rafe had led to her pregnancy. Fine, she'd earned that one herself. But everything else?

She was tired of doing the best she could with what she got, because what she got was crappy. That's all there was to it. Her parents dying? That was a crappy thing that happened when she was at that age where she needed her mother more than anything. But she went on. She didn't go to Harvard, didn't go out into the great big world and find her own place in it, as Mac had gotten to do. Instead, she stayed home and became a damn fine ranch manager.

But did she get to fall in love? Every boy she'd ever liked had been chased off by Mac. And now there was Rafe. She didn't know if this was love or lust or hormones or what. She liked him. She was definitely attracted to him. And she was going to have his baby. But was that love? Or was this just another crappy thing that was happening to her, another thing she was going to have to muddle through as best she could?

Could she convince Mac that she could handle this,

handle her life? Would he keep trying to shield her from the real world while inadvertently setting her up for the exact heartbreak he was always trying to prevent in the first place?

If he had just bought the Wild Aces when he had the chance…

Angry tears stung her eyes, but the agitated mooing of calves and cows reminded her that she was not, in fact, in the privacy of her room. Instead, she was out on the ranch, surrounded by cows and cowboys, and she was the boss.

That's right, she was the boss. She needed to act like it. She looked up at the sky, trying to get all of her hormone-enhanced emotions under control. She could not fall apart, not now, because if she did, she'd lose the Wild Aces.

Wildly, she thought of Rafe. Where was he? She needed him right now in a way that she wasn't sure she'd ever needed anyone before. For so long, she'd been struggling to show that she was fine, that she could take care of herself. But right now, she wanted Rafe to pull her into his arms and tell her that it was all going to work out, that he'd take care of it—of her. God, she'd never wanted that so much.

And he wasn't here.

"Violet?" Dale asked, worry in his voice. "Everything okay?"

She turned back to where Dale was dusting his chaps off. The other hands were looking at her with confused concern. To them, she was just another cowboy. They didn't treat her like a porcelain doll the way her brother did—but the downside of that was, if she ever had a more emotional moment, they didn't know what to do. It was as if being suddenly reminded that she was, in fact, a woman always freaked them out.

She was not freaking out. She sent a quick text to Rafe, asking him where he was, and then she got her boss face on. Losing the Wild Aces wasn't just a crushing blow to her long-held dream. It could easily be a crushing blow to the Double M. The only reason Mac had agreed to lease the Aces was because they had multiple springs on the property—springs that had remained undamaged from the tornado that swept through Royal last year.

"The Wild Aces might be sold out from under us," she said, keeping her voice level.

Dale whistled and the other cowboys almost visibly relaxed at the revelation that Violet wasn't going to start crying. Because she wasn't. Absolutely no crying in baseball or ranching. "That's gonna put us between a rock and a hard place," Dale said.

"We can..." She had to prepare for the worst-case here—losing the Wild Aces completely. "We can lease Taggert's land and..."

Dale shook his head. "He sold out to Samson Oil a few months back."

"What about—"

"Samson Oil," Dale cut her off. "All of them. The Aces was the last holdout, and Lulu only hung on for as long as she did because she's got a soft spot for you."

"What the hell?" Violet stared down at her phone again, as if it somehow held all the answers. Did Samson Oil own it all? By God, she was so tired of having this crap happen to her. This was the last straw. "I have to talk to Mac."

She would make that man see reason and if they had to shell out $1.5 million damned dollars to get the Wild Aces, then that was his fault for not listening to her the first time. She was the boss. It was high time to show her brother that.

"We've got this," Dale said, motioning her toward her horse. "Go on."

"Thanks, Dale." Violet mounted Skipper and lit out for the house. She was so upset she couldn't even fret about whether or not Rafe would give her a look for riding hell for leather.

They couldn't lose the Wild Aces.

Now she just had to convince Mac of that fact.

"Well, howdy, Violet." Mac's assistant looked up from her desk. "We don't see you during the day much—is everything okay?"

"Andrea—I need help." That was the understatement of the day but Violet's throat closed up and for the second time in the past twenty minutes she was on the verge of tears. Luckily, Andrea Beaumont was one of her closest female friends—not to mention the only person who could get Mac to do anything, basically.

Andrea's face got serious and she stood up, quickly moving around the desk to put her hands on Violet's shoulders. "Oh my God—what?"

As she looked into Andrea's caring face, the corners of Violet's mouth pulled down and her eyes began to water and dammit, she was this close to crying. "I'm going to lose the Wild Aces," she managed to say.

"What? Oh, honey," Andrea said, relief washing over her face. "Good heavens, you scared the heck out of me." Andrea pulled Violet into a quick hug. "I thought there was something seriously wrong. You looked lower than a rattler belly in a wagon rut."

Something was seriously wrong. "I—" *I'm pregnant.* But the words wouldn't come out. She couldn't spill the beans just yet—not without talking to Rafe again. She quickly corrected course. "I'm just worried. We need the Aces for water and if it's sold..."

Andrea sighed. "I wish we could have gotten him to buy it when he had the chance. If you'd come to me first, maybe..."

"Yeah, I know." Mac would never take a suggestion Violet made at face value. He'd only hear her asking for the frivolous things she asked for as a kid—a new pony, new boots, more toys. He never believed that she could have an idea that had merit.

But she'd wanted the Wild Aces so much that, instead of waiting around for Andrea to massage the message, Violet had barged right into all the reasons the Double M should acquire the Wild Aces over dinner. What a mistake that had been.

And now that mistake was going to cost her almost twice the price Lulu would have sold her the Aces for a year ago.

Well, this wasn't all her fault. If Mac wasn't so damned convinced she was nothing but a foolish girl, he'd have seen the logic behind her request and bought the Wild Aces in the first place.

Of course, this was an emergency. There was no time to let Andrea work her magic. She had less than a day to convince Mac that the Aces wasn't just another frivolous thing she wanted—it was part and parcel of the Double M's survival. "Is he in?"

"Yes, let me check." Andrea knocked on Mac's door and stuck her head in. "Your sister is here."

"Come on in," Mac said in the background.

"Good luck," Andrea whispered as Violet edged into the room.

"What's up, sis?" Mac asked without looking up from his computer.

Was there a good way to start this conversation? No, there wasn't. The best she could do at this point was keep quiet about her pregnancy for as long as she could. If Mac found out now—in the middle of this whole thing with Samson Oil—well, the situation would get muddled up beyond all hope. At the very least, she wanted her doctor's appointment to happen before she told Mac.

"We need to buy the Wild Aces," she said without preamble.

Mac sighed heavily, as if she were twelve all over again, an irritating little sister he could barely be bothered to humor. "Again with the Wild Aces, Violet? We don't need to waste money on land we don't need."

"But we need the water, Mac. This isn't about what I want. This is about the Double M. Lulu called—some outfit named Samson Oil offered her two million for the Aces. She'll give me twenty-four hours to come up with at least one-point-five but otherwise, we're out. And if we're out, we'll be out the water."

"Wait—did you say Samson Oil?"

"Yeah, I did. And Dale said they've bought up the Taggerts' land and all the other ranches around ours. If we don't meet Lulu's offer, we're going to be locked out, Mac. We need the water or we'll lose the Double M." She was proud of the way she kept her anger out of it.

Because if he'd just listened to her the first time—or all the other times after that—they wouldn't be in this position.

The blood drained out of Mac's face and he sat back, his full attention on her.

"What?" she demanded. Because he looked a lot more upset right now than he had when a tornado had damaged their wells.

"Samson Oil is—well, it's Rafe. I just found out at the

Cattleman's Club meeting. The other night." He looked flabbergasted. "Kyle Wade told us all."

"Wait—what?" For maybe only the second time in her life, Violet felt faint. The first had been when her parents hadn't come home, but Sheriff Nathan Battle had shown up with some woman Violet had never seen before to tell her that she was now an orphan. It had been perfectly understandable then that Violet had fainted.

But this? Rafe *was* Samson Oil?

Yeah, this was as good a time as any to feel light-headed.

"Hey—hey!" Mac jumped up and hurried toward her. "Geez, Violet—what the heck? Sit down," he said, his voice thick as he caught her under the arms and guided her to the chair in front of his desk. "Andrea, get some water!" he shouted.

"I'm fine," Violet lied, because she wasn't sure of anything anymore, except that she wasn't fine at all. She had just plumb run out of coping, thank you very much. No coping left at all. She couldn't handle one more shock to the system.

Mac grabbed a manila folder off his desk and began fanning her. Andrea rushed in with a glass of water and the two of them hovered over her like protective mother hens. "Should we call an ambulance?"

"For the love of Pete, I'm fine," Violet said, more forcefully this time. She was the boss. Not her emotions and not her hormones. "It's just...he didn't mention Samson Oil when we had dinner."

And that seemed like a rather important fact. When he said he'd look into the Wild Aces for her, for example—that would have been a great time to mention that he was behind the corporation buying up all the land surrounding the Double M at insane prices.

Wait—maybe she was looking at this wrong? What if Rafe had done exactly what he'd said he was going to do?

Hope flared through the mess that was her head. Maybe he was buying the Aces for her, just as he'd said?

"Well, he is Samson Oil," Mac went on. "He didn't deny it at the meeting or anything. Instead, he just said that he was exploring mineral rights." Mac stood back up, frowning. "I don't know, Violet. I mean, it's Rafe—but there's something about this that's not right."

"Dale said we'd be cut off from the water." Just as soon as the hopeful thoughts that Rafe had really bought the Wild Aces for her had emerged, they were sunk under a crushing wave of worry. "Mac," she started, a sense of horror dawning in her mind, "what if he's *not* here because he's checking in with his old friend?"

Just saying those words out loud made her feel ill all over again.

"I don't know if I can believe that either," Mac said, starting to pace. "I mean, he's only been in Texas for, what? A few weeks, tops?"

Violet opened her mouth to correct him because she knew—intimately—that Rafe had been in the area much earlier than that. Four months ago, in fact.

But that's not what she said, at least not directly. "If he's Samson Oil, and Samson has been buying up property all around Royal since last fall, why didn't he come over months ago?"

And that was the $10,000 question, wasn't it? Why had Rafe been in Holloway four months ago? Where had he been since then? And why was he buying up what basically amounted to half the town of Royal, Texas?

"I don't like this," Andrea said quietly. But she wasn't looking at Mac when she said it. Instead, she was staring at Violet.

Oh, no. Andrea wasn't exactly a mother figure, but she was the closest thing Violet had to a big sister. And if anyone could look at Violet and see the little changes that had been happening to her—and put all those little changes together to figure out the one big change—it'd be Andrea. The woman's attention to detail was almost inhuman.

Violet knew her eyes were wide and yeah, she was pretty sure she looked guilty because Andrea's eyes got wide right back. Too late, Violet realized she had covered her stomach with her hands and not in the going-to-be-sick way but the cradling-my-pregnant-belly way. Mac had missed the gesture entirely. But Andrea hadn't.

Oh, *no*. Andrea's mouth opened to say something but Violet cut her off with a shake of her head. They could not have this conversation right now, in Mac's office of all places. Not happening.

Andrea gave her what could only be described as a stern look before quickly nodding her head in agreement. "We'll talk later?" she said quietly.

"Okay," Violet said because really? She wanted to tell someone and of all the people in the world, Andrea was not only the safest option but the one who could most help Violet share her "impending blessing," as Rafe had called it, with Mac with minimal collateral damage. If her mom were here, Violet would have already cried it out on her shoulder. Andrea was the next best thing.

Just not here. Not now.

Her phone buzzed. Numbly, she dug it out of her pocket and saw it was a text from Rafe. When can I see you again?

She stared at the phone. Well, this was awkward. But then, her whole life had become one continuous string of awkward moments. She better get used to it. Where are you?

In Holloway at the inn. Thinking of you.

If she hadn't just been questioning Rafe's every motivation for being in the greater Texas area, she might have been touched by that sentiment. We need to talk.

The problem was how to talk without Mac finding out. It'd been wonderfully convenient that he'd been away on a business trip a few days ago but now? What excuse could she use to get Rafe alone?

Violet looked up at Andrea. "I need Mac to be busy tonight," she said in an urgent whisper.

"Why?"

Violet bit her lip. "I'll explain later."

Andrea gave her that stern look again. "Later, we're going to talk."

"I know. But tonight?"

Andrea sighed heavily, then stood and turned her attention back to Mac. "We need to talk with the other landowners who've already sold to Samson and get an idea of what the terms of the sales were and see if they were all told the same thing or if there are inconsistencies. Once we have a little more information, then we can consider approaching Rafe."

God bless that woman, Violet thought.

Her phone buzzed again. Are you still there?

"Yeah, okay," Mac said, rubbing the back of his neck. "Something doesn't add up, I tell you." He turned his attention back to Violet. She barely managed to get her phone flipped over so her screen was pressing against her thigh before Mac saw. "You going to be okay?"

"I'm fine, really," she said again.

"I want you to go home and take it easy for the rest of the day. Maybe Andrea can come by and fix you some chicken-noodle soup?"

Violet gave Andrea a look, one that Violet hoped said, *Keep him busy.*

"I think I need to come with you," Andrea said carefully. "Violet says she's fine and besides, two heads are better than one. I'll take notes while you talk to people."

"Okay, yeah, that sounds good." When Andrea relaxed into a smile, Violet thought she saw something unfamiliar flicker across Mac's face. "We'll get some dinner and make an evening of it. If," he added, glancing at Violet, "you're sure you're going to be okay?"

Violet stood, casually tucking her phone back into her pocket. "Mac," she said carefully, "I'm not a little girl anymore. If I say I'll be fine, I'll be fine."

For a second, she thought Mac was going to argue with her. But Andrea stepped forward and said, "She'll be fine, Mac."

Mac turned his attention back to Andrea. That look came over his face again and he said, "All right," as if he were physically incapable of taking Violet's word at face value.

God, she loved her brother, but sometimes she just wanted to strangle him.

Violet knew she shouldn't press her luck. She should quit while she was—okay, maybe not ahead, but at least not falling further behind. But they still hadn't resolved the whole reason she'd come here today. "What about the Wild Aces?"

Andrea shot her a warning look. Right. Violet needed to let this drop and she needed to let Andrea work her magic when she and Mac were making an evening of it, so to speak.

"Let me talk to a few people," Mac said, grabbing his hat and firmly cramming it on his head. "But Violet—I won't let it go without a fight. Not if Rafe's got some ulterior motive."

Andrea nodded, and although Violet desperately wanted to remind Mac of how very much they needed the Wild Aces, she let the matter drop.

As soon as Mac and Andrea were safely in his truck, with Andrea already on the phone making calls to everyone who had sold to Samson Oil, Violet texted Rafe back. I'm here. When's good for you?

Now, was the immediate response. Shall I come to you? Or you to me?

She had promised Mac she would go home. And as long as she and Rafe stayed downstairs—with their clothes on—if Mac came home, she could just say, well, Rafe dropped in to chat about all this Samson Oil business.

Can you come to the house? she texted back.

I am on my way.

See you soon.

Soon she would know what he was up to and what part she played and whether or not she was going to get the Wild Aces.

God, she hoped this worked out.

Nine

Rafe paused only long enough to procure another rose for Violet, and even with that small detour, he made it to the Double M in record time.

He did not see Mac's vehicle, which was good. In the two days since he'd left Violet's bed, he hadn't been able to stop thinking about her.

It was discomforting to realize that he missed her. Worse, though, was the fact that he was having conflicting thoughts about the property she wanted, the Wild Aces. The purchase was going according to plan. Despite the issues that kept cropping up, victory was still within his grasp. Once he had the Wild Aces, he could choke Mac McCallum off his property. Revenge served very cold indeed.

Except that he kept thinking back to the grand old home on the Wild Aces, and how Violet wanted to make it over and raise his child there. And how Rafe wanted very much to give her just that—to give her whatever she wanted.

That insidious voice in the back of his head that sounded like his father's angry shouting berated him for even considering letting the Wild Aces—and his entire scheme—fall apart for the sake of one woman.

The family honor. The family name. No one uses a bin Saleed like that and gets away with it.

That was what his father had shouted after he had come to collect Nasira and found her in Mac's bed. Those were the very words he had used to shame Rafe for allowing some common American to take advantage of a bin Saleed.

That was why Rafe was here. That was why he now owned half of this county. He had to avenge the family honor.

In all respects, Rafe had been surprised that his father had not taken even more drastic measures against Mac and his family. But to do so would have continued to draw attention to how Rafe and Nasira had so badly betrayed the family honor. Better to keep the whole incident quiet. At least, that was what Fareed had managed to convince the old man.

Rafe had to do something. The years between when his father had walked in on Mac and Nasira, and the old man's death had nearly killed Rafe in a very real way. All because Mac did not respect Rafe or Nasira enough to keep his lust in check.

Rafe was a bin Saleed.

Honor. Revenge.

Violet…

The diamond-and-ruby bracelet felt heavy in his pocket. It was all part of his new-and-much-improved plan. Wooing Violet away from Mac would complete his revenge in ways he had not even originally considered. He was not letting his scheme fall apart. He was expanding upon it.

As he mounted the steps onto the wide porch, Violet opened the door and he knew immediately that something was not right. "Are you well?" he asked, hurrying to take her in his arms.

"Rafe," she said, not exactly melting into his embrace. Instead, she stayed stiff and he heard the tension in her voice.

And her text came back to him: We need to talk.

He leaned back and looked down at her. And he knew, somehow, that she'd discovered his scheme.

Was it weakness that he wanted to delay that confrontation, even for a moment longer? Was it weakness that had him pressing his lips against hers for one more kiss, because after this kiss, he did not know if he would have another chance to hold her in his arms?

Or was it just the fact that he had failed and he sought the comfort only Violet could provide?

She did not kiss him back. Not as she had kissed him the last time he had seen her.

Suddenly, Rafe was nearly overcome with the urge to fall to his knees and beg her forgiveness. Once, Violet McCallum had been an abstract concept, an afterthought to his scheme. But now? Now she was a living, breathing woman who had shared herself with him, body and soul, and he had been careless with that. With her.

"Who are you?" she said, her voice soft. But that softness did nothing to disguise the anger that she was barely keeping in check. "Who are you, really?"

"Rafiq bin Saleed," he told her truthfully. "I sometimes use Ben. It was…simpler."

"Simpler?" she scoffed, turning away from him.

"Easier to pronounce," he offered, trailing after her as she stalked into her home.

"Or just easier to hide who you really were?"

"That, too."

She spun, her eyes blazing. "Tell me how you're involved with Samson Oil. Tell me why you were here four months ago. Tell me why you suddenly seem to own every single piece of land surrounding the Double M." She began to advance on him and, thankfully, years of conditioned response from being berated by his father had Rafe standing his ground. Cowering was bad enough but to cower before a woman?

"And tell me, Rafe," she went on, her voice getting louder with each word, "*tell me* it doesn't have a damn thing to do with whatever happened between you and Mac back in college. That 'it does not signify.'"

By this point, she was standing directly in front of him and poking him in the chest with one of her fingers.

Tell me you have not failed me. The words were not Violet's but his father's. It had been a trap, because of course Rafe had failed him and Nasira. Rafe had failed the country of Al Qunfudhah by foolishly trusting a duplicitous American.

Some part of him knew that he had failed Violet, that she had had nothing to do with what happened between Mac and Nasira, that she had nothing to do with the hell on earth that had come afterward.

But that part was buried deep beneath Rafe's survival mechanisms. And Violet, while formidable, was not Hassad bin Saleed.

He straightened his back and leveled his best glare at her. He was not the same wayward youth. He would not be dressed down by anyone anymore. Least of all a woman.

Not even *his* woman.

Rafe pushed her finger away from his chest. "Ah, so you have figured it out, have you? I should have guessed that you would put the pieces together before your idiot brother did."

His words had the desired affect—the color drained from her face and, off balance, she stumbled backward. "What?"

Without thinking about it, he caught her around the waist to keep her from falling. He didn't tuck her against his chest, however, nor did he attempt to comfort her. He kept distance between their bodies. "Sit, please. I have no wish to see you hurt."

"Figured *what* out, Rafe?"

"Sit, Violet." This time, it was not a request. It was an order. He backed her up until she hit the chair with the backs of her legs and sat with enough force that Rafe winced. "Take care. Please, think of the child."

Violet looked down at her stomach as if she expected an alien to emerge from her body at any second. "The... child? You still..." Her voice trailed off with the unspoken question.

"Yes, of course I still want the child. The baby will be my flesh and blood just as much as it will be yours." Rafe took the sofa where he had been sitting when she first walked back into his life. She had been ready to flay him alive then. Some things, it seemed, would never change. "Now. Tell me what you know and what your brother knows."

She blinked at him and slowly, he could see her regain her control. "You are Samson Oil."

"That is correct."

"And you've been buying up all the ranches surrounding the Double M for months. That's why you were in Holloway four months ago."

Rafe nodded. "You are correct. I have also bought quite a few other parcels of land."

She looked at him in what he could only call surprise. "Why?"

"So as not to arouse suspicion."

He saw her swallow. "Oh. Of course. And…the Wild Aces? Were you going to buy that, as well, before I told you about it? About how much I wanted it?"

He felt a dull ache spreading in his chest but he held his pose, leg crossed over his knee, arms spread out along the back of the couch. He took up as much space as he could. "Yes."

Pain tightened her features to the point where Rafe fought the urge to stand and pull her into his arms. The jig, as they said, was up. "So you weren't going to buy it for me?"

He let the question hang in the air until he was sure he had his foolish impulses to comfort her under control. "Originally, no."

"Originally?"

"I will keep it for you. In a few years, after this is all settled, you may have it."

He would not have thought it possible for her to get any paler, but she did. "A…few years? And this—what *is* this, Rafe?"

The urge to move was almost overwhelming. No, he did not want to back away or run and hide, but even to stand and pace would be a physical relief. But with his father, any such betrayal of his mental state had always led to not only more beatings, but more severe beatings, as well. So Rafe forced himself to be still. "You are quite bright, Violet. Do not tell me you have failed to guess what 'this' is."

"Mac," she said. It came out almost as a croak.

He nodded his head in acknowledgment. "I can be very patient. Twelve years was nothing to me, not after what your brother did to us."

"But—he didn't," she sputtered. "He told me he found your sister in his bed and that he never even touched her. He always felt terrible about it, but it wasn't his fault!"

Rafe looked at her coolly. "And you believed that, did you?"

Her mouth opened and shut. He could read the doubt in her eyes. "Mac wouldn't lie to me. Not like you do."

"Don't be naive," Rafe said, his tone condescending.

This was not happening. It couldn't be. Maybe... maybe Violet really had fainted in Mac's office. And she was still unconscious. That'd explain this.

The man she was sitting across from looked like the same man she'd met in Holloway months ago. The man she'd taken back to her bed in the past week.

The man she had started to fall for.

But he wasn't. He was nothing but a cold, heartless bastard. "How could you do this to us?" she asked, although she was already starting to get a pretty good idea of the answer. "How could you do this to me?"

Her throat started to close up and her eyes began to water, but she wasn't going to cry. She wasn't going to give him the satisfaction of knowing how upset she was. Besides, she figured a snake of a man like Rafiq bin Saleed wouldn't be moved by a woman crying anyway. That would imply that he was capable of emotions.

He sat looking at her for what felt like a very long time. "Because," he said slowly.

"Don't give me that, Rafe. *Because* isn't an answer. Why are you doing this to me? I never did anything to you or your sister. I never even knew you."

It was only when Rafe exhaled—long and slow, the kind of controlled breath that seemed to say to her he was barely in control—that she realized he might not be quite as calculating as she'd gathered. So she did what she always did—she spoke. Impulsively. "Was this your evil plan all along? Were you waiting for me in Holloway that night for the express purpose of getting me pregnant? Am I nothing but a pawn to you?"

"I understand if you hate me," he said in a much softer voice than she had been expecting.

"Hate you? Jesus, I don't know if I should shoot you or not. And don't think I don't know how," she spat at him. "Talk, damn you."

"You may choose to believe what you wish to, but I have not lied to you."

A bark of laughter escaped her. It was either laugh or start sobbing, and she was the boss of her emotions right now, thank you very much.

"I have, it is true, omitted many things," Rafe went on after she'd settled down. "I did not know who you were—that was the truth. I promised to use a condom, and I did. I promised I would not contact you outside of that evening, and I did not. I promised I would look into the Wild Aces, and I did. Honor is everything to my people, and my family and I have made every effort not to dishonor you through lies."

"You'll excuse me if I don't exactly see the difference between you lying and you carefully not mentioning that the whole reason you were in Holloway and Royal in the first place was to destroy my family."

The infuriating man waved his hand, as if she were

splitting hairs, but he didn't have the energy to argue with her.

"My revenge is complete, with your assistance," he said. He tried to smile, but even in her upset state she could see how forced it was, as if there were something that were pushing him to say and do these awful things. "Surely you can see how Mac and I will be even. He ruined my sister. I merely returned the favor."

Where was her gun? Oh, that's right. Up in her room. She'd never make it up and back before Rafe could get out of range. Dammit.

"For your information, I don't think your sister was ruined just because she chose to get into bed with my brother, and I don't think you ruined me just because I chose to sleep with you—which, by the way, will never happen again."

"As is your choice," he said and there was no mistaking the sorrow in his voice.

"If you think you're ever going to get our baby, you're wrong. I'll fight you every step of the way."

"It does not have to be like that," he said, and it might have been her imagination, but she swore he looked worried.

Well, he could just be worried. She surged to her feet, letting the anger carry her. "The hell it doesn't. I won't let you get the Wild Aces, I won't let you get the Double M, I won't let you get my baby and I sure as hell won't let you get *me*. Now get out."

Rafe stood. "It is too late, you realize. The Wild Aces is as good as mine and soon, your brother will not be able to sustain the Double M."

"It ain't over till it's over," she retorted. "Now leave before I get my gun."

He nodded and walked to the front door. Then he

paused and turned back to her. "You should have been a pawn," he said mournfully. "But you were not. It gives me no pleasure to do this to you."

"Then don't," she said, unable to believe what she was saying. "Don't do it to me. Don't do it to us." And she was horrified to realize that she wanted him to do something—what, she didn't know. Something that would show her that underneath that imperious exterior was the real man she'd almost loved.

"There is no us," he said, turning away from her. "And I have no choice in the matter. I am bound by honor and obligation. But I will hold the Wild Aces for you and for our child. I promise you that, Violet."

She needed to say something—get the last word, put him in his place, but all she could do was watch him open up the door to her house and close it behind him when he went.

Then she sank into the chair and cried.

But not for long. The Double M was her ranch, her home. She was the boss around here. She did not have time for self-pity.

She dialed Mac. "I need you to come home right now," she told him when he answered. "We need to talk."

By the time Mac and Andrea rolled in, Violet had gotten herself under control. She'd texted her best friends, Clare and Grace, because if there was one thing she needed right now, it was backup. She'd splashed her face with water and had a ginger ale and was, all things considered, feeling up to the fight.

"What?" Mac demanded when he walked through the door. Violet stood and faced her brother. "What's so important that you couldn't tell me on the phone? Did you find out something about Samson Oil or Rafe?"

Andrea put a gentle hand on his shoulder and made eye contact with Violet. "What is it, Violet?" she asked, her gaze dropping to Violet's belly.

"Okay, I've got a couple of things to say and I'm going to say them," Violet said, trying to remember to breathe.

"All right," Mac said, looking worried. "What?"

"First off, I'm pregnant."

That might not have been the best way to go about this, but Violet was done tiptoeing around Mac. *"What?"*

"Second off," she said, charging ahead, "Rafe is the father."

"What?" Mac roared. "That bastard! I asked him to keep an eye on you and this is how he repays me? I'm going to—"

Violet held up her hand and Andrea squeezed Mac's shoulder and miracle of miracles, the man shut up. "Third off, I'm four months pregnant. Actually, four months and almost two weeks."

Mac's mouth opened and then shut again. "Wait, what?"

"Rafe was in town months before he showed up here, claiming he wanted to reconnect. I met him at the Holloway Inn in November. That's where..." Mac blanched. Okay, they didn't need to get into the details. "Anyway, I needed a night out. I didn't know who he was and he claims that he didn't know who I was, although obviously we can't exactly take him at his word right now. It was a one-night stand that didn't go quite according to plan."

"Oh, honey," Andrea said.

"I don't think I want to hear anymore," Mac said, looking a little green around the gills.

"Fourth off, he's out to get you and, as near as I can figure, I'm just collateral damage. He made me a lot of promises over the course of the last week and he swears that he'll hold on to the Wild Aces for me and I can have it in a few years after he's put the Double M out of business."

"So this is all—what, exactly?"

"Revenge," Andrea said. "This is revenge."

"She's right. He said he was honor bound to get you back for ruining his sister. Originally, that just meant ruining you. But I guess I provide the ironic twist, don't I?" Her voice cracked and Andrea pulled her into a big hug.

"It's okay, honey," she said softly.

"How the hell is this okay?" Mac shouted. "Some insane sheikh is out to ruin me because his equally insane sister decided the best way to get out of a bad marriage was to be caught in my bed? I had nothing to do with any of this!"

"Mac!" Andrea hissed. "Now is not the best time!"

Mac looked at Violet, who was sniffing violently. "I'm—oh, God, I'm sorry, Violet. I didn't think…"

"It's okay. But I have one more thing I want to say." She straightened up and pushed herself out of Andrea's arms.

Mac eyed her warily. "What's that?"

"This—if you had bought the Wild Aces when I asked you to, if you had listened to me at any point in the last twelve years—we wouldn't be in this position."

The man had the nerve to look hurt. "But Violet—I was just trying to protect you. You've had to deal with more than your share, what with us losing our parents and—"

"It's been twelve years, Mac. I'm not a little girl anymore and I'm not the shell-shocked teenager I was when you got home from college. I'm a grown woman and a ranch manager and soon I'm going to be a mother. Everyone else knows that I can handle myself—even this surprise pregnancy, I can deal with it. But I've spent years tiptoeing around you and asking Andrea to convince you to do things for me because every time I open my mouth, you act like I'm just the cutest little thing playacting at adulthood and I'm sick of it. I don't need your protection. I'm not just your little sister. I am your business partner, dammit, and it's high time you started treating me like it."

Mac gaped at her but, amazingly, didn't tell her he was going to handle it or that it was all going to be okay. "Well, then, what do you suggest?"

Luckily, she'd had enough time to think through the next step. "The only way to cut Rafe off is to buy the Aces out from under him. Lulu said she'd sell it to me for one-point-five million. The very last thing I will ever ask of you is to help me buy it. We need the water and I need my own place to raise my family."

For a second, she thought maybe she'd gotten through to the big lunkhead, but old habits died mighty hard, because Mac's gaze cut to Andrea. Violet rolled her eyes, and she saw Andrea's lips twist into something of a knowing smile.

"She's right," Andrea said. "You know she is."

"Dang it all, I know." Mac took off his hat and rubbed his forehead. "I don't know if we can beat him to the punch. No one knew who was behind Samson Oil at first and the money was too good. He had Nolan Dane doing all his negotiating for him. Kyle Wade is the one who outed him, but I don't think any of us saw this as revenge. Except for you," he added before Violet could correct him. "And why didn't you tell me you were expecting?"

"Because the moment I figured it out is literally the moment Rafe showed back up and I had a lot to deal with, okay?"

Mac put his hands up in the universal sign of surrender. "Okay, okay. Sheesh."

"I need the Wild Aces, Mac."

He nodded—slowly at first, but then more emphatically. "Then I'll go get it for you, partner."

Ten

"I don't know what I'm going to do." It was all well and good for Violet to stand up in front of her brother and tell him she could handle this, but now, far away from Mac, she wasn't so sure.

Which was how she found herself at the Royal Diner, sitting with her best friends, Clare Connelly and Grace Haines, and pouring her heart out while Mac went to try to get the money by liquidating some capital—or something like that. Violet did not handle the money end of things, so Andrea had gently suggested that she get together with her friends for a little girl time.

Violet really did love Andrea. The woman was a peach.

"Honey," Clare said, slinging an arm around Violet's shoulder and giving her a firm hug, "if anyone can handle this, it's you."

"But I'm pregnant." Now that Violet had said the

words out loud, she seemingly couldn't stop saying them. She'd been telling friends, neighbors, Dale—even random people she met in the street. She was pregnant and she was screwed.

"You keep saying that like it's the end of the world, but you know it's not," Grace said. "Heck, I'm suddenly mother to twins. It's a lot but it's *not* the end of the world. You've survived worse, you know."

Violet was too emotionally drained to even wince. "Yeah, but my parents' plane crash was a one-and-done event. This? The father of my child is basically out to destroy the entire town of Royal because he's nursing a grudge against my brother about something that happened over twelve years ago. This isn't a one time trauma. This has the potential to be an ongoing international incident. I mean, he's a sheikh, for God's sake!"

Clare and Grace shared a look. "I'm sure something can be worked out," Clare said. "I mean, look at Grace. First she was Maddie and Maggie's social worker and now she's going to adopt them and marry their father..."

"What Clare is saying is, just because it's complicated doesn't mean you can't find a way to make it work," Grace finished.

"And you know I'll be here with you," Clare said, giving Violet another squeeze. "I love babies! I'll teach you everything you need to know and when your baby gets a little older, we can all have playdates together."

"We?" Violet and Grace both turned to look at Clare. Grace said, "Is there something you're not telling us?"

Clare blushed. "Actually, I'm pregnant. But!" she said quickly, hushing her friends before they could start whooping and hollering. "I'm only a little pregnant. Probably not more than five weeks along, so we're going to keep it quiet for now, okay?"

Now it was Violet's turn to hug Clare. "Oh, honey," she said, and damn the stupid hormonal tears that started up again. At least this time, they were happy tears, right? "I'm so excited for you and Parker!"

As they were comparing due dates, the chimes over the door jingled. All three of them looked up at the newcomer. A woman with long, thick black hair wearing a beautiful gold-yellow suit glided into the diner as if she were walking on rose petals—which was impressive, given her heels. Those suckers had to be at least five inches tall and yet this woman moved in them as if they were a natural part of her feet. The woman paused inside the door and removed her hat—not a cowboy hat, like most of the people here wore, but a short, wide number that was the exact color of her suit, complete with a feather that swept out over the huge brim.

All in all, she looked like someone who might have gotten lost on her way to a royal wedding and wound up in Royal, Texas, completely by accident.

And Violet recognized her immediately.

"Wow," Clare said in a hushed whisper.

"Beautiful," Grace agreed. "Who is that? She's not from around her, is she? I'd remember the hat."

"Rafe," Violet said. Both the women turned to look at her. "I mean, she looks like Rafe. Excuse me."

Her heart pounding, Violet slid out of her booth and approached the newcomer. What was Nasira bin Saleed doing here? Rafe had promised that he would try to arrange a meeting between Nasira and Violet—but Violet was pretty sure Rafe had said he didn't think Nasira would come to America. "Hi—Nasira?"

Because who else could she be? Looking like this woman did—the black hair and olive skin and the same nose and chin as Rafe?

The woman's face registered surprise. "I am sorry," she said in an accent that was similar to Rafe's, but very different. Whereas Rafe's voice always made Violet think of warm sunshine and honey, this woman's voice sounded almost like...like rain and fog and mist. It was not an unpleasant thing, but it was very unexpected. "Do I know you?"

Violet stuck out her hand. "I'm Violet McCallum. I'm Mac's sister. And you're Rafe's sister, Nasira—right? You look like him."

Nasira blushed. "Ah, yes. Violet. Hello. How fortunate I have found you so quickly. I have come to warn you and your brother that—"

"That Rafe's going to buy up the entire town and ruin Mac?" Nasira winced. "Yeah, sorry—it's kind of too late for that."

Nasira clutched at her hat and paled. "Oh, no—I am too late? What has he done?"

Violet decided she liked Nasira immediately. "Why don't you have a seat? Would you like some coffee? Then we can talk."

Clare and Grace introduced themselves and Nasira politely said hello, although she did not shake hands. "Well," Clare said, standing and giving a knowing look to Grace, "we best be running along. But Violet—you call us the moment you need anything."

"Anything at all," Grace added.

And then Violet was alone with Nasira. Once the other women were gone, Nasira sat in the seat Grace had vacated. She sat very stiffly, her back straight and her chin up. She placed her fancy hat on the table next to her and waited silently while Amanda Battle, the owner of the Royal Diner, poured the coffee.

"Anything else I can get you all?" Amanda said, trying not to stare at Nasira.

The Royal Diner was pretty much ground zero for gossip in this town. Violet glanced around. Luckily, aside from a few stragglers, Violet and Nasira had the place to themselves.

"I think we're good," Violet said, smiling warmly at Amanda.

She and Nasira were silent until Amanda was out of earshot. Then, with the most graceful gesture Violet had ever seen, Nasira leaned forward and said, "Tell me what has happened. What has Rafe done?"

So Violet told Nasira what she knew—about Samson Oil, the land grabs, the Wild Aces, everything but her relationship with Rafe. She doubted if just casually blurting out that a person's brother had gotten her pregnant after a one-night stand was "done" in Al Qunfudhah. Violet's life might be a total scandal, but she didn't need to add fuel to the fire if she could help it.

When she'd finished, Nasira sat back—again, her back ramrod straight—lowered her eyes and said, "This is my fault. I am so sorry for the trouble I have caused."

The resignation in her voice alarmed Violet. "What? No way. I mean—okay, so something obviously happened twelve years ago. But I fail to see how that makes you personally responsible for what's going on here."

She was horrified to see Nasira's eyes tear up. "I brought your brother into a family problem without explaining it to him. It was unfair to him and unfair to Rafe."

"Yeah, so what exactly did happen back at Harvard? Mac insists he didn't do anything with you and Rafe won't tell me what he thinks happened either."

Nasira's gaze sharpened, just a little, and she again

looked more like her brother. "Are you and Rafe on good terms, then? Does he talk to you?"

Violet realized she was blushing. "You first," she said, trying to play for time. "Your story happened first, so you tell it first."

"All right," Nasira said again, her voice a little cooler this time.

Oh, yeah, this was Rafe's sister. There was no mistaking it.

After a long pause, Nasira leaned forward again, her voice soft—no doubt to keep anyone from overhearing them. "I chose Mac precisely because I knew him to be an honorable man who would not violate me," she explained. She picked up a packet of sweetener and began to fiddle with it—the first sign of nerves that Violet had seen yet. "I know that may sound unusual to your American ears, but at the time, I felt that letting my father believe I had been compromised by a man such as Mac was the only way I could escape the fate he had chosen for me."

"A man such as Mac? I don't understand—obviously, your father didn't see him as an honorable guy."

A hint of color graced Nasira's cheeks. Really, everything the woman did was grace embodied. "No, he did not. My father barely tolerated Rafe attending an American school, and Mac was not of royal blood. So to be 'defiled' by him—or so my father believed," Nasira hurried to add when Violet opened her mouth to argue with that particular assessment, "was lowering myself even more."

What was it with these people? Ruined? Defiled? No wonder they were so screwed up. Did they ever fall in love and have sex simply because they wanted to?

There had been that night, many months ago, when Violet had gone to bed with Rafe because she wanted to.

She'd wanted one night of fun and freedom and—yes—good sex. And Rafe? He had wanted all those things, too.

But did he now view her as ruined? Defiled? Had he lowered himself by making her pleasure his?

Ugh, she was nauseous again.

Nasira had dropped her gaze to the table, so she missed Violet's reaction. "You must try to understand. I was to be wed to a horrible man, a man I feared greatly. He was well over sixty and had already had two wives who had died in 'accidents' that were not accidents. His first wife died because she only gave birth to girls and his second…well, I do not know why."

Violet gasped. "How could your father marry you off to such a man?"

Nasira looked at her sadly. "I hope you can understand how different our families are. This was all expected when I was a child. I had been promised to the warlord for some time. He was a powerful man and my father wanted to keep him close. It was only when Rafe left for university in America and met your brother…" Her voice trailed off. "Rafe told me such stories, you see. And the way he spoke of his friendship with Mac, of you—of this place—it was almost too good to believe. For the first time in our lives, I envied Rafe."

Violet gave her a confused look. "Wait, what? I mean—you were going to be married off to a monster and you didn't already envy Rafe?" How did that even make sense?

Nasira gave her that sad smile again, one that spoke of pain that Violet could only begin to fathom. "Rafe is second in line for the sheikhdom. In England, he would be the spare, as they say. But we did not grow up in England and my father treated Rafe harshly."

Violet stared at her. Harshly? How harshly?

"But I am getting off the point," she went on. "Rafe was in America and having all of these wonderful adventures, and I was envious. I managed to convince my father that, for my eighteenth birthday, I should be allowed to visit Rafe. Our older brother, Fareed, took my side. It was he who told me what Rafe was doing here in Royal," she added.

"Okay, so Fareed is a decent guy?"

"He is *not* our father," Nasira said emphatically. "He is a just and fair ruler of Al Qunfudhah."

Well, that had to count for something. "So you got to visit Rafe in America and while you were here, you decided to get out of the marriage by… Is *seducing* the right word?"

Nasira's eyes widened in horror and she shook her head. "No, no. I had convinced your brother to kiss me by explaining my situation but, at the last moment, I feared that would not be enough, so I made a foolish choice and snuck into his bed. That was where our father found me." She dropped her gaze again and went back to mangling the sweetener packet. "I regret that choice, but please understand, I also do not regret it. What came after was…terrible." She shuddered and Violet shuddered in sympathy.

"You didn't have to marry that guy, right? That's what Rafe said. He said you were able to leave Al Qunfudhah and marry a man more to your liking."

"Sebastian, yes." There was a note of sorrow to her voice that she tried to hide with a smile. "My life has been much easier than I had ever allowed myself to dream it could be. However, I do not believe Rafe's was." She didn't speak for a moment and, for once, Violet managed not to open her mouth and charge into the gap. "It was a relief when our father died and Fareed took power," Nasira said quietly. "Rafe was allowed to resume life in the outside world."

Violet felt herself gaping at Nasira like a catfish out of water but she couldn't quite get her face under control. "You make it sound like your father imprisoned him because he didn't protect you. Or your honor, anyway."

"It sounds that way because it was that way." Nasira's words were little more than a whisper. "I believe that, in the years between my actions and our father's death, Rafe held one thought that sustained him. And now that he has regained his power and his wealth by his own hands…"

"Revenge."

Nasira set the sweetener packet down and returned her hands to her lap. Violet could see her composing herself. "For a long time, I've wished that there had been another way. It is all my fault."

What Violet needed was a drink. Of course, she couldn't exactly wander over to the bar and do a line of shots, no matter how much she might want to block out the world for a while. "Well. This certainly puts a new spin on things."

"Oh? And what about you, Violet? You speak as if you know Rafe."

"I do. I…" She took a deep breath. "I don't really know how to say this without it sounding bad, so I'm just going to say it. I'm pregnant and Rafe's the father."

She wasn't sure what she expected Nasira to do with that bit of information, but bursting into tears and smiling at the same time wasn't it. "Nasira?"

Amanda Battle hustled over. "Is everything okay?"

"Um—tissues?" Violet said. Just watching Nasira cry was making her tear up, too.

Amanda hurried back behind the counter, bless her heart, and reappeared with a box of tissues. "Thanks,"

Violet said. Amanda got the hint and retreated back to the counter.

"My deepest apologies," Nasira said, grabbing a tissue and blotting at her eyes. "It is just…well, I am very happy that Rafe has opened himself up. I had believed that part of him might have died after…"

"But you're crying," Violet said gently.

"It is nothing," Nasira said, which was pretty obviously a bold-faced lie. "I am quite happy for you and for Rafe," she repeated.

"But…"

Nasira tried to smile but she didn't make it. "I have long wanted a child of my own and we have not been blessed with one. Sebastian is an honorable man. He wishes to have an heir and I…I cannot. I recently lost the baby I was carrying and now he will not…" Her voice trailed off with such hopelessness that it almost overwhelmed Violet.

"Oh." This time, Violet didn't even try to rein in her own tears. "I'm so sorry. This must be—oh," she repeated numbly. Because seriously, the fact that she got pregnant after one time had to be salt in the wound.

"Please," Nasira said, drying her eyes and putting on a good face, "do not apologize. Tell me more of Rafe. You are aware of his scheme, yes?"

"I figured it out. And when I confronted him about it, he told me the rest. I just…look, I get that he blames Mac. But it's been twelve years. And your father—how long has he been dead?"

"Almost seven years," Nasira said.

"Why is he still doing this? I thought…" Now it was her turn to look down at the table. "I thought he cared for me. But when I confronted him, he told me that Mac had ruined you and he was just returning the favor."

Nasira gasped in horror. "He said that?"

Violet nodded. "And I feel like such a fool because he made all these promises that sounded so good, about how I would always have a place in his country and how our child would be both a bin Saleed and a McCallum and…and it was all a trap. He didn't care for me, but I fell for him."

Unexpectedly, Nasira reached across the table and took Violet's hand in hers. "Do not think such things," she said, a harder edge to her voice. "I know Rafe and I know he does not say such things lightly. He does not allow himself to grow close to people in general and women specifically. That was what was so unusual about his friendship with Mac. I do not think that, before that time, Rafe had had many friends"

"Really? But he's so charming. Too charming," she admitted.

"I shall speak to him," Nasira said decisively.

"What? No, you don't have to do that."

"Please," Nasira said, but it wasn't a request. It was an order, and Violet remembered that, touching moments aside, she was technically sitting across from royalty. "This whole thing began with me and will be ended by me. Rafe has no just cause to treat you like this."

"I just don't want my baby to be this rope in a tug-of-war between me and Rafe," Violet said. "I don't want to keep his child from him but I can't live in fear that he'll take my baby and disappear into the desert and I'll never see my baby again."

"I will not allow it," Nasira said. "And if Rafe attempts such madness, Fareed will step in. You will be the mother of a bin Saleed. That affords you certain rights and protections, both in Al Qunfudhah and I assume here in America."

Violet nodded. "I mean, I guess. I haven't even seen a doctor yet. Everything's happened so fast..."

And what she really needed was for things to slow way, way down. At least long enough that she could get a handle on the situation. Honestly, at this rate, she was becoming numb to the shocks. She wouldn't even be surprised if the ghost of Rafe's dad, the old and seemingly really cruel sheikh himself, floated into the diner. It wouldn't faze her at all.

She glanced toward the door. Well, maybe not too much, anyway.

"Do you know where Rafe is?" Nasira asked.

"He's been staying at the Holloway Inn—it's about thirty minutes from here," Violet said. "That's where we met the first time."

Nasira brought up the inn's information on her phone. "Ah, I see."

"What about you? Do you have a place to stay? Do you want to see Mac?"

Nasira blushed, and in that moment, she looked much younger—probably more like the girl who'd been so desperate for a way out that she'd do anything. "He wouldn't be happy to see me, not after what Rafe has done," she said quietly. "I shall take a room at the inn where Rafe is."

"Will you call me and let me know how it goes?"

"Of course."

They exchanged numbers and Nasira stood to go. "Thank you," she said, putting her hat back on her head.

"For what?" Violet asked, trying not to be jealous of Nasira's style and grace. God knew Violet couldn't pull that level of class off. The one time she'd tried, well, she'd ended up pregnant.

"For caring about Rafe. He needs that more than you

could ever know." Her face took on a battle-ready look. It was a beautiful battle-readiness, but still, Violet decided that, in a throw-down, she'd put her money on Nasira. "I will not let him destroy this chance."

"I don't know that I care for him anymore. Not after all of this."

Nasira gave her a smile that sent a shiver racing down Violet's back. "We shall see."

Then Rafe's sister swept out of the Royal Diner just as quickly as she'd arrived. Violet glanced back to where Amanda was trying hard to look as though she wasn't listening. "Not a word to another living soul," she said.

"Not a word!" Amanda held up the Girl Scout sign. "On my honor!"

Violet sighed. She needed to warn Mac that the plot had thickened yet again. But she sat there for a little bit longer, trying to make sense of everything Nasira had shared. Realistically, she knew it was possible that Nasira was here because Rafe had called her, that she was a hedge against damage control. If Rafe's plan blew up in his face, he'd want a soft, beautiful woman to help with the public relations disaster.

Violet had already been a fool more than once, but she couldn't help but feel that Nasira was being honest with her. The woman's reaction to Violet's pregnancy had been too raw, too real.

And if Nasira was being up front, then it followed that…

Rafe's father had gone far beyond punishment. Rafe had spent literal, actual years planning this revenge. He claimed it was for Nasira's honor but…

She wasn't going to care. Rafe's history was tragic, but that didn't excuse his behavior now. He was single-handedly trying to ruin her family, her business and nearly the entire town of Royal, Texas. Violet needed to focus on protecting herself, her assets and, above all else, her child. Rafe wasn't even on that list.

So why did she hope that Nasira could talk some sense into him?

Yup, she was just that big of a fool.

Eleven

The Wild Aces was his.

True, it had cost Rafe an additional million dollars, but three million was nothing when he was worth a thousand times that. Three million dollars was nothing compared to the satisfaction of having finished what he set out to start.

This was a moment of victory. Years of planning and biding his time had finally come to fruition. Rafe had finally, finally avenged his family's name and honor.

He owned the Wild Aces.

He owned Mac McCallum.

Yet…

As Rafe sat in his car outside the Holloway Inn, he could not help but wonder if this was really what victory was supposed to feel like. That dull pain in his chest was back and had been ever since Rafe had dragged the real estate agent away from her family during dinner and driven madly through the countryside to get to the Wild Aces.

That pain had only gotten stronger when, coughing hard, Lulu Clilmer had told him she'd promised Violet McCallum twenty-four hours in which to match Samson Oil's offer. That was when Rafe had made an offer Lulu could not refuse—provided, of course, she signed the papers right then.

It had taken all of his self-control not to order the woman to sign. But in the end, a warm smile and obscene amounts of money had done the job for him. Lulu had signed.

Rafe should celebrate this victory. But the moment that thought occurred to him, his mind turned back to Violet—to meeting V in the bar of this very hotel and taking her to his bed. Promising that her pleasure would be his and then keeping that promise. Taking her to dinner at Claire's and waking up in her arms. Going for a ride across the Texas grasslands and watching her rope a wayward cow and feeling that, for once in his life, he was at peace. He'd glimpsed what happiness could mean for him—not as a distant, undefined thing he would never know, but a real thing he could hold in his hands when he held Violet close.

He was not at peace now. And he wasn't sure why. This was what he wanted, after all. Exacting his revenge upon Mac was the very thought that had kept him going during those dark years. Ruining Mac's life just as Rafe's had been was everything he had been working toward. His work here was about to be done.

Except that Mac had welcomed Rafe back with open arms, even vouching for him to his friends. Except Nolan Dane had been the closest thing Rafe had had to a true friend since Mac's betrayal. Except for Violet and the child she carried.

What was it about these people, this town, that made him doubt himself? No, this was not doubt. He was a bin Saleed. He did not have doubt and he did not question his motives. His motives were pure. The code he lived by—the code that had governed his family for generations—required this. Rafe had damaged the honor of the bin Saleed name. Retribution was the only way to restore that honor.

It was unfortunate that Violet had become a part of the scheme, he thought dimly as he exited his vehicle. And it was unfortunate that Nolan had lost sight of the larger goal and turned his back on Rafe.

It was unfortunate that they had all turned on him, but it did not signify. All that was left to do here was to confront Mac and let him know that Rafe had been the source of his downfall and that justice was finally served.

Then Rafe would be on the family plane, headed back to Al Qunfudhah. Back to the stretches of sand that backed up against the deep blue of the sea. Back to the family home, where Fareed ruled and Rafe was, once again, an unnecessary second. Back to where happiness was an unknown, unknowable thing that was not for him. Never for him.

It was fine. Rafe would turn his full attention back to the shipping business. Piracy was a growing concern and he needed to take measures to prevent his ships from being hijacked. If he could keep his costs low, he could undercut his competition and increase his share of the market, which would in turn increase the standard of living in Al Qunfudhah. That was how his time would be best spent. That was how he was most useful to his people. His personal happiness and sorrows did not signify. He felt nothing.

The pain in his chest was so strong that he paused outside the sliding doors of the Holloway Inn. Had it only been a matter of months since he had walked through these very doors and seen *her* sitting at the bar, the black lace of her dress contrasting with her creamy skin? Since he had taken one look at her wide smile and beautiful face and decided that he needed her in a way that he had not allowed himself to need another person?

Had it only been that long since he had given a part of him to her—a part he had not realized was his to give?

He rubbed at his chest, but it did nothing to help. He needed to leave this accursed place, he decided. In the morning, he would seek Mac out and then he would leave. He needed to be far, far away from Royal, Texas, and the people in it: people who made him want to care about them, people who seemed to care about him.

None of them did. Mac had not cared enough to keep his hands off Nasira. Nolan had not cared enough to stand by Rafe's side when he met a woman. And Violet…

Well, she had cared. Perhaps too much. More than was wise. And he had made her hate him.

At least she hadn't shot him.

One more day. He would be gone by this time tomorrow and then he could begin again. Perhaps Fareed would have selected a wife for him and he could produce legitimate heirs. That had been the purpose he had been raised for, after all. He would visit his wife when appropriate and the children would be shown to him by their nannies in the evening, as was proper. He would hardly know they were there.

And his child here…

Don't do this to me. Don't do this to us, Violet had

whispered, and he had wanted so desperately to turn back to her, to take her in his arms. In that moment, it didn't matter if it was a sign of weakness, but he could not inflict this pain on her. Not willingly.

But really, what choice did he have?

Still, he did not have to keep hurting her. No, he decided, he would not take the child from Violet. Her only crime was being Mac's sister—that and opening herself to him. There was no just cause to hurt her for that.

A voice in the back of his head—a quiet voice that sounded nothing like his father's—whispered that perhaps there was no just cause to hurt her at all. Perhaps, this soft voice suggested, there was no just cause to hurt any of them. Not Mac, not Nolan, not Violet and not the town of Royal.

Rafe pushed this thought aside. That was weakness talking and he had not come this far only to let doubt destroy everything he'd worked for. He'd spent years planning for this moment. This was not the time to have cold feet, as the Americans said. If anyone knew he was filled with this hollow pain, they would use it against him.

Rafe forced himself to breathe regularly. Years of his father's abuse had taught him that the only way to survive was to be as impervious as stone, no matter what Hassad had said or done to him.

Rafe was that stone now. Nothing could hurt him. Not even Violet's stricken face or the way she had cradled her stomach, seemingly without even being aware she was doing it, while she told him she would fight him at all costs.

It did not have to be that way. He had no wish to treat his child as he had been treated. Just the thought of his own flesh and blood having to survive what Rafe had survived at the hands of his father made his stomach turn.

Rafe focused on the movement of each breath in and out of his body. It would not be that way, not if he had anything to say about it. Perhaps, after some time had passed, he could return for a visit or he and Violet and the child could meet somewhere neutral. New York, perhaps. He could give her the deed to the Wild Aces and see his child and that would be enough for him, to get a glimpse of that happiness again, to be near it. He had made do with far less.

Perhaps he could, perhaps he could not. But could he really do that to Violet?

What happened to him did not matter. It never had. But what happened to her—to their child—could he really do this to them?

There had to be a way. He had to do something to protect her and the child, to show her that he cared for her. Something more than just holding the Wild Aces for her.

He could not destroy her. But this was weakness. If his father were still alive, he would beat Rafe for his weakness until he had no more skin left on his back, but he didn't care.

He had to show her she was not the pawn in this game—that she was something more. Much, much more.

This thought calmed him and he was able to straighten up. He would find a way to shield Violet and, until such time as he did, he would continue on. This happiness with Violet was separate from his revenge on Mac.

Besides, it would not do for Sheikh Rafiq bin Saleed to be seen staggering into a hotel as if his heart had been ripped clean of his chest. He was victorious. He had damned well better act like it.

When he was in full control of his faculties, he walked through the sliding doors of the inn. Habit had him scanning the lobby. He had been doing it for months now—

every time he returned to the inn, in fact. And he was always looking for the same thing—his beautiful, mysterious V.

His gaze came to rest on a woman, sitting stiffly in a cushioned armchair facing away from him. With a start, he realized he recognized that posture, that hair, that regal bearing.

Not V. Not Violet.

Nasira.

His sister was here? He had not seen her in several years, although they communicated via email on a regular basis. He was so stunned by her sudden appearance that he had to pause and think—had he called her here? He remembered promising Violet that he would arrange a meeting between the two women. But that was back when Violet was still speaking to him, and Rafe had been so busy in the interim that he was certain he had not had the time to summon Nasira.

Rafe did not allow himself to feel uneasy about this development. There was nothing to feel uneasy about, after all. This was merely his sister, the woman he had promised to protect. The woman he had failed. The woman whose honor he was avenging at this very moment.

"Sister," he said. He had always called her that instead of using her name.

"Ah, Brother, I see you are looking quite well." She rose gracefully to her feet and smiled. "Texas, it seems, agrees with you."

Rafe was immediately on the alert because he certainly didn't feel quite well. "Sister, why are you here?"

If he had offended her, she did not show it. Instead, she tilted her head to one side and gave him a piercing look. "Are you not glad to see me?"

"But of course I am." He stepped forward to wrap his arm around her shoulders and press a kiss to her cheek. "Does Sebastian know you are here? Are you well? Are you…" He glanced down at her stomach.

That got a reaction out of her. As Rafe watched, he saw her eyes grow flat and he knew that his question had caused her pain. For so long, she had been struggling to have a child with her husband. To ask such a question so baldly was in poor form. "Forgive me," he said gently. "That was unkind."

"Never fear." She put that sunny smile back on her face, but it didn't reach her eyes. "We are much the same. He is aware I am here."

Something about that admission sounded off. "Will he be joining you?"

Color bloomed on her cheeks. "Ah, no."

Rafe and Nasira were not children anymore, but to see her embarrassed in public brought back uncomfortable memories, and an old instinct to shield her from attention kicked in. "Shall we continue this conversation in my room? Or your room—are you staying here? I do not even know how long you plan to be in Royal. I intend to leave tomorrow, but if you are here, I do not see why I should not stay with you. I am sure that Sebastian would feel better knowing you are well cared for."

Again, she tilted her head to one side. "I am sure that Sebastian would appreciate that, if he knew you were here. And as for how long I am staying, that depends, I suppose. But yes," she went on before Rafe could ask what, exactly, she meant by that. "It would be best to talk in private, I believe."

"This way." He led her to the elevator. As the doors closed, he felt another unfamiliar stab of panic. "I must ask, Sister—how did you know where I was?"

"Fareed informed me," she said, but she did not elaborate.

"I am glad to see you. In fact, I had thought about calling you several days ago."

"Oh?" She turned to him. "Was there a reason?"

This was his sister, after all. He was not any more comfortable lying to her than he was lying to Violet. "You were in my thoughts," he said, which was both the truth and not exactly the truth.

She tilted her head. "I am honored."

Finally, the elevator came to a halt on his floor. He led the way down to his room and unlocked the door in silence.

Nasira swept into the room, but she did not take the office chair, nor did she sit on the edge of the bed. Instead, she stood in the center of his room as if it were hers, her hands folded in front of her. "So, brother," she said once the door was shut and he was facing her. "Tell me how you came to be here in Royal, Texas."

What had Fareed told her? "I could ask the same of you."

She waved this away. "I am here because Fareed gave me good reason to think that you are here for less-than-honorable reasons."

"I can assure you, sister, my reasons for being here are entirely honorable." It came out harsher than he meant it to. He did not speak harshly to Nasira. He protected her. He tried anyway.

And wasn't that really why he was here? He had tried to protect her and failed.

She sighed heavily, as if his statement had inspired nothing but disappointment. That was how she looked at him—with disappointment. That hollow pain in his chest bloomed again, burning with emptiness. "It is as we feared, then."

"What is?" He was the stone. He felt nothing because feelings were weaknesses and weakness was not tolerated. He was a bin Saleed.

"It began with me, so it shall end with me." She squared her shoulders and fixed him with a fierce gaze. "I was a virgin when I married Sebastian."

"What?" The statement caught Rafe so off guard that he recoiled a step.

"I never slept with Mac McCallum," she went on, as casually as if they were discussing the weather. "Nor did he even know I was in his bed that day. He had agreed to kiss me in front of our father to help me escape the fate that awaited me, but I was young and foolish and impulsive." She favored Rafe with a sad smile. "So foolish. I was afraid that a mere kiss would not be enough to dissuade our father, so I hatched a different plan. I snuck into Mac's bed when I knew you would be showing Father how you lived."

A strange numbness overtook Rafe's limbs as the scene played out in front of his eyes again.

Nasira had been nude under the covers, all of her clothing in a pile on the floor where they would be impossible to miss. Her hair had been freed of its braid. She had looked exactly like a woman awaking in her lover's bed. "We found you there. In his bed."

"Yes, I had been counting on it. My dear brother," she said in a voice that was almost pitying, "you are not the only one in this family who is capable of great schemes."

"Why are you telling me this? Why are you lying for him again?"

There was no mistaking the pity in her eyes this time. "Why do you persist in believing that I am lying for him?

I tried to tell you on the plane ride back. I did not want to marry that monster Father had assigned me to. I did not want to be forced into any marriage against my will. And to that end, the scheme worked perfectly. But I had not foreseen the other consequences. I did not realize what Father would do to you. And worse, I did not realize that you would do this, Rafe. I never dreamed you would even be capable of it."

"You don't know what you're talking about," he snapped at her. "You have no idea."

"Oh?" She was unruffled by his anger. It only made him madder.

"Everything I have done, I have done for you. For your honor. For our family name."

"That is why I have come to stop you."

"Are you quite mad?" he roared.

"Are you? You are the one who has nursed this perceived hurt for years. Years, Rafe. I understand that you are bitter that Father treated you like a prisoner in our home. I regret every day that my choice led to such dire consequences for you. That is a burden I carry with me everywhere I go."

He opened his mouth to say something—what, he did not know, but something, dammit all, that made her realize that *bitter* did not even begin to describe him. But she held up a hand, cutting him off with all the commanding manner of a member of the royal family. "But I have never given up hope for you, Rafe. You are not our father. He is dead and I am glad of it. You no longer have to do as he would do. You no longer have to prove that you are as cruel and heartless as he was."

"This is not cruelty," he shouted, unable to get control of himself. "Cruelty is being thrown in a dungeon and beaten because I allowed my friend to defile my sister."

"Cruelty," she calmly responded, "is destroying a man and an entire town because you were beaten. Cruelty," she said, her voice rising in pitch, "is destroying a woman who cares about you, a woman who carries your child even as we speak." Her voice cracked, the first true sign of emotion since his words had wounded her earlier. She put her hand on her heart. "Cruelty is being given the gift of love, of a child, and doing everything within your power to destroy those gifts."

He would not be moved by her sorrow. "Mac betrayed me!"

"No, Rafe. No." She shook her head and regained her composure. "The only person who has betrayed you is you. Well," she added in a casual tone, as if she had not just swung a hammer of words at his stone heart and broken it to small bits, "you and our father. But then, he betrayed us all, did he not?"

Rafe stared at her, unable to form words in his mind and equally unable to get his tongue to say them.

"Fareed is worried about you," she went on in a quiet voice. "We all are. We had hoped that, with Father's death, you would have been able to find peace. You have a chance for that, Rafe. Do not be the man Father demanded you to be. Be the man you want to be."

She moved a chair out of the way and walked toward him. No, not toward him—toward the door. When she reached him, she said, "Please forgive me for my part in your pain. It was never my intention to see you hurt. But believe me when I say this—I will fight to protect your child from you, if it comes to that. The choice is yours."

She stepped around him. He heard the door open and then shut. He knew, at least on some level, that he was alone.

But he was not. Ghosts of the past—and the present—

cluttered his vision. He saw Nasira in bed, looking shocked to have been discovered. But now he remembered that she had disappeared from their group only a few minutes before that—thirty, at most. Not nearly enough time to have slept with Mac in his bed.

And Rafe remembered Mac's shock at coming into the room and finding all of them there like that—Nasira in his bed, Rafe standing next to it, Hassad raging at both of them. At the time, Rafe had taken that shock as confirmation that Mac had not expected Hassad to find him with his lover but…

Was it possible he had been just as shocked about seeing Nasira in his bed?

And then it had all happened so fast. Within hours, they were on the family jet, flying back to Al Qunfudhah.

"Tell me you have not failed me," Hassad had said in that dank dungeon, in between blows. And Rafe had known there was no hope. He could not defend himself, for his father would call him a liar and beat him more. And he could not admit defeat because his father would beat him for being a coward.

And Fareed—he was there, as well, sneaking down to the dungeon with extra food or wine, with medicines that took the edge off the pain or a blanket to make the stone floor more comfortable or books to read so that Rafe did not go out of his mind. "I will convince him," Fareed had promised. "This is not your fate."

And Rafe had been so beaten down that he had not bothered to correct his brother. This was his fate. He took his father's anger so Hassad did not treat his other children this way. That had always been Rafe's fate, ever since he was a child and had defended Nasira, his closest sibling, from Fareed's teasings and had gotten slapped across the face for daring to speak against the future sheikh of Al Qunfudhah.

Rafe had not gotten to see Nasira get married to Sebastian, a man who did not beat her and did not use her poorly. He had not gotten the chance to meet the man for years.

And Nolan Dane—his ghost was here, as well, looking at Rafe with distrust and something verging on horror.

Then there was Violet—his beautiful, mysterious V, his tough, quick cowgirl. She was carrying his child. She had been haunting his every thought for months. Did he honestly expect that he would return to Al Qunfudhah and not see her everywhere he went?

And woven in with all of these visions were past versions of himself. Of the boy who took the beatings so his siblings would not have to. Of the young man who attended to his tutors closely and dreamed of leaving Al Qunfudhah behind. Of the man who was ripped from his studies and his friends. Of the scarred man who refused to cower in the face of the abuses heaped upon him by the one person who was supposed to have defended him. Of the determined man who watched and waited and schemed.

Of the man who'd seen a beautiful woman who had sparked something in his chest, something that had not been there before. Something that made his heart cry out for pleasure, for something *more*.

Something more. That was what Violet was to him. More than just revenge. More than the stone wall he hid his heart behind. More than what his father expected and demanded.

With a cry of pain, he realized what he had become. Mac, Nolan and Violet—most especially Violet—they had opened their arms to Rafe, embraced him as friend and family. He had never been a sheikh's second son, not to them. He had always been Rafe and, for the first and only time in his life, just being Rafe was enough. More than enough.

Rafe would never be enough for Hassad bin Saleed. He could keep trying and trying and trying but the old man was dead and gone, and just as Nasira had said, Rafe was glad of it.

But he had been wrong. He thought that with Hassad's death, he had been freed of the old man. But he saw now that he had still carried Hassad with him, allowing his father's perverse sense of honor to warp Rafe's thoughts and actions.

Mac had been blameless. And in the name of a dead man's honor, Rafe had bought almost half an American county's worth of land to ruin his old friend.

Nolan had offered Rafe friendship but the moment he got too close, Rafe had shut Nolan out and driven him into the arms of a woman who would love him.

And Violet… She was beyond blameless. Yet Rafe had used her poorly. Cruelly, even.

What had he done? Hassad was dead. Yet he still controlled Rafe. Perhaps that had always been the old man's scheme, his plan to live from beyond the grave.

Well, no more.

Rafe had much work to do.

Twelve

Only one window at the McCallum house spilled light out into the night. It was not Violet's window—of that, Rafe was certain. Did that mean Mac was the only one home?

It did not matter. Rafe was here to make things right and if that meant he had to go through Mac, then that was what must be done.

Rafe shut his vehicle off and got out. Before he even closed the car door behind him, the front door of the McCallum house burst open.

Ah. He would have to go through Mac. Fitting.

But as Mac came down off the porch, Rafe drew back in alarm. He had never seen Mac this visibly angry before. His hands were balled into fists and, for the first time, Rafe thought his old friend could physically harm him.

The question that remained unanswered was, would Mac pummel him for what he'd done to Mac—or to Violet? It did not matter much. Either way, Rafe was deserving of this fury.

Despite the rage that poured off Mac in waves, Rafe held his ground. Years of habit had trained Rafe not to fall back or seek cover. Instead, he awaited his fate.

"Give me one good reason," Mac growled as he advanced in long strides, "why I shouldn't shoot you where you stand." Though he didn't have a gun that Rafe could see, the threat hung heavy in the air between them.

Because if Mac had a gun and pulled the trigger, Rafe would not survive. But he would not fight back.

The family honor, his father's voice whispered insidiously. *No one uses a bin Saleed like that and gets away with it.*

But this time, Rafe pushed the thought away. He did more than push it away. *No one uses a bin Saleed like you used me*, he thought back. *And I am not your instrument any longer.*

Mac was staring at him, rage and confusion blending into one hard mask of hatred. Rafe had earned that. "Well?" Mac demanded.

"You always were a man of honor," Rafe said, not bothering to hide a smile.

"Not like you, you dog. You and Violet? And the land? Why?"

Rafe took a breath. He suspected he had only one chance to get this right. "I have come to beg your forgiveness."

"I'm not buying that load of bullshit." Rafe did not flinch. That instinct had been beaten out of him years ago. "All this happened because you thought I slept with your sister. But I never even touched her, dammit."

"So she has told me."

The confusion in Mac's eyes overtook the rage a bit. "What?"

"She is here. Well, in Holloway. My brother told her

what I was doing. She came to make things right." Odd, that after so many years of trying to protect his siblings, they were now the ones doing the protecting. Except that, instead of protecting Rafe from their father, they were trying to protect him from himself.

"I don't understand."

"She has explained to me what happened the day we found her in your bed," Rafe went on, still trying to make sense of the day's events. "And I have realized something."

Mac fell back a step. "Yeah?"

"I came here for revenge." There was no cushioning that truth with soft words. "But I did not come here to avenge her. I thought I had. I thought I was meting out justice for the shame you brought upon my family's honor and our name. But that was a lie, I see now. A lie that justified my actions."

Mac took another step back. "So why are you here? Why did you come?"

Rafe found himself looking up. The stars were clear and bright here. When his father had him trapped in the dungeon, he had hardly seen the night sky for years. *Years*. "I came here to avenge myself."

"I didn't do a damn thing to you," Mac said. "And I'm not going to let you destroy Violet. I'd sooner rot in prison than see you ruin her."

Rafe smiled at this. "A man of honor," he repeated quietly. "I understand. For, you see, I did the same thing."

"What?"

Rafe had that weird out-of-time sensation again, the same one he felt when he had gone riding with Violet and slept in her bed with her. "I think it was always supposed to be this way," he told Mac.

"I don't know what you're talking about."

He grinned. "I am in love with your sister."

Before Rafe could protect himself, Mac stepped forward and punched him in the jaw. Rafe was knocked sideways as pain bloomed in his face, but he kept his feet underneath him. All told, he deserved that punch.

"You have one hell of a way of showing it. You hurt her, you ass. I've done everything I could to protect her and you waltz in here and..." His voice shook. "And you hurt her. She doesn't deserve that."

Rafe straightened. "No, she doesn't. But you can't get revenge for her." He took a deep breath. This was right. This was peace. "You can only get revenge for yourself."

"What?"

"I have hurt you, Mac. We were friends—I considered you to be a brother. Which makes the way my entire family acted toward you all the worse." Rafe bowed his head before Mac. "Please accept my apologies on behalf of my sister, my father—and myself. You did not deserve to be used like you were."

Mac stood there, his mouth open wide as he gaped at Rafe. "I—you—"

"I would like to speak to Violet now." Rafe reached for the deed to the Wild Aces. "I want to give this to her and tell her I love her."

But as he moved, Mac tensed and reached behind his back. Someone screamed.

And a gun went off.

"That bastard is here." Those had been Mac's exact words as he'd grabbed his pistol, shoved it in the back of his waistband and run out the door before Violet could do anything else.

Rafe had come back? That man must have a death wish. If Mac didn't get him, Violet would.

Lulu had called. She was sure sorry, but three million—well, she knew that Violet would never be able to come close to that. The money was too good. She'd signed the papers.

Tears silently streaming down her face, Violet had ended the call.

Gone. It was all gone. All because Rafe had his facts wrong.

Bastard wasn't a strong enough term.

Still, she didn't exactly want Mac to shoot Rafe. At the very least, he shouldn't kill Rafe. A flesh wound might be okay.

No, that was just the anger talking because if Mac shot Rafe, Mac would wind up in prison and Rafe's family would want to know why and there would be an international incident. And the very last thing Violet wanted right now was an international incident.

So she hurried out through the kitchen and crept along the side of the house, sticking to the shadows. When she could peek around the porch, she saw that Rafe and Mac were standing only a few feet away. Oddly, Mac wasn't holding his gun. Odder still, the two men were talking.

"...And tell her I love her," she heard Rafe say as he reached into his pocket.

Mac tensed and reached around his back—for his gun.

Oh, God—he was going to shoot Rafe. And Rafe had just said that he loved her? Hadn't he?

One thing was clear. Mac couldn't kill Rafe. He couldn't even wound him.

But that wasn't stopping Mac. He had the gun out of his waistband. She tried to shout a warning—but she couldn't even get the words, "Don't kill him!" out before a shot was fired into the darkness.

Violet screamed so loudly that the world went blue on the edge of her vision and then, just as it was going black, she saw both men turn in her direction.

Rafe was the last thing she thought about before she blacked out.

"Violet," she heard a silky voice say. For some reason, it made her think of sunshine and honey, warm and sweet. "Are you well? Please open your eyes," the voice pleaded. "Please be well."

"Here," another voice said. This one was gruff and tight. It was her brother, Mac.

"Ah," said the liquid sunshine voice. *Rafe*. Rafe was here. Oh, thank God.

Then something wet splashed on her face and she startled. Her eyes flew open and she saw the night sky and Rafe's face close to hers and Mac's hovering behind him. "What happened?"

"Someone scared the hell out of me," Mac said. He sounded mad, but she could see the worry lines on his face. "And I pulled the trigger."

"I fear the car will never be the same," Rafe said. He managed a small grin at her.

"You're not dead? I'm not dead?"

"No one is dead," he assured her. "You, however, fainted."

"Dammit." This was embarrassing.

"Yeah," Mac replied. "She's shooting her mouth off again. She's fine. Help me get her up."

"I have her," Rafe said. He pulled Violet into his arms and cradled her against his chest. Then, as if she weighed nothing at all, he stood. "If you could be so kind as to find the paper I dropped…"

"Sure. What is it?"

"The deed to the Wild Aces." He said it casually as he carried her into the house.

"What?" she gasped.

"The Wild Aces. It is yours." He sat down on the couch, but he did not let her go. Instead—in the middle of the living room, in full view of her brother and anyone else who might wander through—he pulled her onto his lap. "Whatever you choose, I will accept. But the land—and the water—it is yours."

She blinked up at him. "Are you serious? You're just going to *give* me the Aces? You spent three million dollars on it!"

"I would pay twice that if that was what it took to give you a beautiful home where you can raise our child. I want you to give him or her the kind of life that you have had, surrounded by family and love."

"I don't understand." It came out confused and weak, and she didn't want to be weak in front of him. She tried to shove herself off his lap, but his arms closed around her and there was no escaping him.

"I am sorry," he said. "I beg your forgiveness, Violet." He gave her an oddly crooked smile. "If my father could see me begging a woman for forgiveness..."

"Don't," she said. "I don't want to ever hear his name again."

"A sheikh of Al Qunfudhah does not ask for forgiveness. And begging is unthinkable. But that is what I am doing now, Violet. I treated you poorly and there is no excuse."

There was something else going on here and it wasn't just that he'd been crazy enough to tell an armed-and-dangerous older brother he was in love with her.

It was the same *something else* that Violet had seen in Nasira's eyes when Nasira had said that their father had imprisoned Rafe. At the time, she had hoped that the other woman was speaking metaphorically or Violet had misunderstood because of the language and cultural differences between them, even though Nasira spoke perfect, if British, English.

What if…what if she hadn't been speaking metaphorically?

Rafe bowed his head over her. "My father was…a difficult man."

Violet waited. She had the feeling that he was getting to the truth of the matter and she could not rush him.

"He held me responsible for what had happened to Nasira. He washed his hands of her and she was able to move to London. In that, I had succeeded in protecting her. Her life has been much better for it. But as for my father, I had failed him. And he made me pay for that failure."

"What do you mean, he made you pay? Nasira said…"

The sorrow on Rafe's face made her eyes tear up. "He locked me in the dungeons."

"Oh, God." She blinked, but the tears refused to go away.

"For years, until he died, I was a prisoner in my own home." His voice wavered and he closed his eyes, but only for a moment. When he opened them again, he looked almost unmoved by what had happened. But she could see now that it was a lie. He wasn't incapable of emotions. He was just hiding the pain. "Fareed is the only reason I am still alive. He snuck me food and medicines and did his best to convince our father to free me—or at least treat me better."

Violet's heart about broke. *Oh, Rafe.*

"It does not excuse my behavior," he said sternly. "But during those years, there was but one thought that sustained me. I had lost everything. My freedom, my life, my friend. And I believed that it was because of Mac that everything I loved had been taken from me."

She didn't know what to say. So instead, she hung her arms around his neck and held him to her, as if that could take the pain away.

Rafe went on, "I told myself that I had to avenge the family name, I had to make us even for Nasira's honor. That was what my father beat into me. But I see now that it was never that. I suffered greatly. And I wanted to make Mac feel the same hopelessness I had felt."

Violet's throat closed up and she had to choke down a sob. So that was it. His father hadn't delivered a metaphorical beating—hell, it wasn't even a single beating. The horrible man had treated Rafe like a whipping boy.

She couldn't stop the tears that traced down her cheeks. All those times when a shadow had crossed his face—was he remembering what his father said or did to him?

This wasn't fair. He was making her feel things for him and she didn't want to. She didn't want to feel anything but hate because he had been prepared to take everything she loved away from her. She absolutely did not want to feel this urge to pull him into her arms and hold him tight and tell him that as long as she lived, no one would ever do that to him again. A silly girl's silly promise—Rafe was a man now, and more than capable of taking care of himself. But, as silly as it was, she wanted to say it to him. She wanted to tell him that she would never let anyone treat their child like that either.

She wanted to keep him safe. After all these years of being guarded and protected, this sudden urge to defend Rafe was almost overwhelming.

Stupid pregnancy hormones. She had no idea if she was mad or sad or upset or so, so happy because Rafe really did love her and he had come back to apologize. He wasn't going to destroy her.

He wasn't going to destroy the two of them.

"All those years ago, Mac had entranced me with stories of your happy family and your beautiful ranch and your town. And for years, I waited for a way to destroy those things. But when I was with you, it all came back to me. And I felt like… I feel like I had finally come home again."

"Oh, Rafe," she gasped. "Why couldn't you see it sooner? I would have been your family. We all would have been. This could have been your home—with me." She lifted his hand and put it against her stomach. "With us."

That look of sorrow passed over his face again, then he cupped her cheeks in his hands and touched his forehead to hers. "I understand. My treatment of you has been unforgivable and I will regret until my dying day that I hurt you so. The Wild Aces is yours, but I know that it can never truly make up for my actions. I will leave tomorrow and I will not trouble you again."

She froze, a feeling of horror building in her chest. "Wait—what?"

Rafe gave her a sad smile. "I wish to stay—I wish to be with you. You are my only happiness. But to do so would bring dishonor upon my family name. But more than that, it would dishonor you and your family. I cannot do that, not anymore. I cannot destroy what I love."

"I swear to God, if you ever talk about doing something stupid out of honor again, I'm going to shoot you myself."

At this announcement, Rafe's eyebrows jumped up so high they almost cleared his forehead. "What?"

"You keep talking like it's too late—well, I've got news for you, buster. Just because you hold a grudge for over a damned decade doesn't mean I have to."

"But—my actions—I have hurt you."

"You're damn right you have." She glared at him, trying to put her thoughts into something that resembled order. "But you've also faced down my brother to apologize. You survived a horrific childhood and yet here you are, trying so hard to do the right thing that you're about to go and screw it up again." She threw her hands up, almost hitting him in the chin. "God! Men!"

Rafe was staring at her, a puzzled look on his face. "What are you saying?"

"You begged my forgiveness. That's what you said, right?" He nodded. "Well, I forgive you. I forgive you, Rafe."

The impact of these words hit Rafe as hard as if she'd actually shot him. He fell back against the couch, clutching at his chest. His eyes went wide and he turned a scarily pale color.

Violet panicked. "Rafe? Are you okay?"

"You—you forgive me?" He said it in such a way that it was clear that the thought had never crossed his mind. Forgiveness hadn't been an option. "I nearly ruined your life!"

"But you didn't," she reminded him. This was right, she decided. She could hold this misguided attempt to rule the world against him—but that would be punishing the son for the sins of the father. And Rafe was more than that.

He was the father of her child. And she would not let those sins ruin them all. "I forgive you, Rafe. I hope you can forgive yourself."

He was physically shaking. She really had no choice but to wrap her arms around him and hold him tight—tighter than she'd ever held anyone before.

"I do not deserve you, Violet. I am not worthy of your love."

"Is that what *he* told you—that bastard of a father of yours? Because it was a lie, Rafe. You are the man I want—when you're not trying to be what *he* wanted you to be."

Rafe looked at her with so much longing and pain in his eyes that she had trouble breathing. "Violet…"

"Found it," Mac said, walking into the room. He took one look at the two of them curled up on the couch together and groaned. "Am I going to have to shoot you or not?"

"In my country," Rafe said without flinching at all, "when a man wishes to marry a woman, he would ask permission of her father or her oldest male relative."

Mac's mouth opened, but Rafe didn't let him get a word in. "However," he said, his gaze never leaving Violet's face, "we are not in my country, are we?"

Violet's heart—the same heart that had very nearly stopped beating only a few minutes ago—began to pound. "No," she said, quietly. "We aren't."

"Lord," Mac scoffed. "I will shoot you if you do anything stupid to deserve it ever again."

Rafe laughed. "I have a feeling you won't have the chance."

"You're nuts," Violet said. "Both of you. Now, Mac—if you don't mind, I think Rafe was trying to ask me something?"

"I don't want to know," he muttered, turning on his heel and stalking out of the room. The last thing Violet caught before the front door slammed was, "…little sister—gross!"

She laughed and Rafe laughed with her. "I'm sorry my brother almost killed you."

"I deserved it. I have no right to ask this of you and you have no obligation to say yes—but Violet McCallum, would you do me the honor of becoming my wife?"

She wasn't sure she remembered how to breathe, but it didn't matter. All that mattered was Rafe was here and there were no more lies between them. "Are you sure we can make this work? You've got to admit that nothing about this has been a normal relationship."

"You have shown me there is another way." Rafe rested his hand on her belly. "I want nothing more than to spend my days riding by your side and my nights in your bed. I want to hear our child's heartbeat and be there when you bring him or her into this world. I want to do all the things my parents did not do, all the things Mac spoke of that gave me hope. Dinners and birthday parties and movies with popcorn and love. I want your love, Violet. I do not deserve it but—"

He didn't get to say anything else because Violet had pulled him down to her and covered his mouth with hers.

"Do you love me?" she asked, pulling away before she lost what little control she still had. "Really?"

"I have never loved anyone before, but I love you. You grace my thoughts during the day and haunt my dreams at night, my beautiful, mysterious Violet. I love you more than I can hold inside me. I think I always have," he whispered against her forehead.

"It was always supposed to be this way," she said, remembering his words. She leaned into his touch, curling her hands into the fine cloth of his shirt and holding him to her.

"I was always supposed to be yours," he agreed. "I just did not realize it until it was too late."

"It's not too late," she told him, throwing her arms

around his neck and hugging him. "But no more shocks, okay?"

"No more shocks. You know the worst of me. All I can hope to do is show you the best of me. Your pleasure is my pleasure," he said into her hair. "And I swear I will spend the rest of our lives giving you nothing but pleasure."

"I'm going to hold you to that," she cautioned him. "Because your pleasure is my pleasure, too."

He cupped her face in his palm and stared into her eyes. "I love you, Violet McCallum. Marry me. Be my family. Because I want there to be an *us*."

Us. He might have torn them apart, but he was going to put them back together. "I love you, too. Stay with me, Rafe. Let me protect you."

"Only so long as I can protect you. This is your last chance, Violet. If you say no, I will leave, peacefully and quietly. I will support our child, but I will not interfere with your life again."

For some reason, she thought of their conversation in the elevator their first night together. He'd given her a chance to say no then, too—but she hadn't. "And if I say yes?"

His grin grew wicked. "If you say yes, you will be mine, you understand? And I will be yours. For always and forever."

"Then I better say yes. I am yours, Rafiq bin Saleed."

He touched his forehead to hers. "I am yours, Violet McCallum."

And that was all either of them said for quite some time.

* * * * *

Don't miss a single installment of
TEXAS CATTLEMAN'S CLUB:
LIES AND LULLABIES
Baby Secrets and a Scheming Sheikh Rock Royal, Texas

COURTING THE COWBOY BOSS
by USA TODAY *bestselling author Janice Maynard*

LONE STAR HOLIDAY PROPOSAL
by USA TODAY *bestselling author Yvonne Lindsay*

NANNY MAKES THREE
by Cat Schield

THE DOCTOR'S BABY DARE
by USA TODAY *bestselling author Michelle Celmer*

THE SEAL'S SECRET HEIRS
by Kat Cantrell

A SURPRISE FOR THE SHEIKH
by Sarah M. Anderson

IN PURSUIT OF HIS WIFE
by Kristi Gold

A BRIDE FOR THE BOSS
by USA TODAY *bestselling author Maureen Child*

* * *

Read on for an exclusive sneak preview of
ONE NIGHT CHARMER
from USA TODAY *bestselling author Maisey Yates*
and HQN Books!

* * *

If you're on Twitter, tell us what you think of
Harlequin Desire! #harlequindesire

Copper Ridge, Oregon's favorite bachelor is about to meet his match!

If the devil wore flannel, he'd look like Ace Thompson. He's gruff. Opinionated. Infernally hot. The last person Sierra West wants to ask for a bartending job—not that she has a choice. Ever since discovering that her "perfect" family is built on a lie, Sierra has been determined to make it on her own. Resisting her new boss should be easy when they're always bickering. Until one night, the squabbling stops...and something far more dangerous takes over.

Ace has a personal policy against messing around with staff—or with spoiled rich girls. But there's a steel backbone beneath Sierra's silver-spoon upbringing. She's tougher than he thought, and so much more tempting. Enough to make him want to break all his rules, even if it means risking his heart...

Read on for this special extended excerpt from ONE NIGHT CHARMER
by USA TODAY *bestselling author Maisey Yates.*

CHAPTER ONE

THERE WERE TWO people in Copper Ridge, Oregon, who—between them—knew nearly every secret of every person in town. The first was Pastor John Thompson, who heard confessions of sin and listened to people pour out their hearts when they were going through trials and tribulations.

The second was Ace Thompson, owner of the most popular bar in town, son of the pastor and probably the least likely to attend church on Sunday or any other day.

There was no question that his father knew a lot of secrets, though Ace was pretty certain he himself got the more honest version. His father spent time standing behind the pulpit; Ace stood behind a bar. And there he learned the deepest and darkest situations happening in the lives of other townspeople while never revealing any of his own. He supposed, pastor or bartender, that was kind of the perk.

They poured it all out for you, and you got to keep your secrets bottled up inside.

That was how Ace liked it. Every night of the week, he had the best seat in the house for whatever show Copper Ridge wanted to put on. And he didn't even have to pay for it.

And with his newest acquisition, the show was about to get a whole lot better.

"Really?" Jack Monaghan sat down at the bar, beer

in hand, his arm around his new fiancée, Kate Garrett. "A mechanical bull?"

"That's right, Monaghan. This is a classy establishment, after all."

"Seriously," Connor Garrett said, taking the seat next to Jack, followed by his wife, Liss. "Where did you get that thing?"

"I traded it. Guy down in Tolowa owed me some money and he didn't have it. So he said I could come by and look at his stash of trash. Lo and behold, I discovered Ferdinand over there."

"Congratulations," Kate said. "I didn't think anything could make this place more of a dive. I was wrong."

"You're a peach, Kate," Ace said.

The woman smiled broadly and wrapped her arm around Jack's, leaning in and resting her cheek on his shoulder.

"Can we get a round?" Connor asked.

Ace continued to listen to their conversation as he served up their usual brew, enjoying the happy tenor of the conversation, since the downers would probably be around later to dish out woe while he served up harder liquor. The Garretts were good people, he mused. Always had been. Both before he'd left Copper Ridge, and since he'd come back.

His focus was momentarily pulled away when the pretty blonde who'd been hanging out in the dining room all evening drinking with friends approached the aforementioned Ferdinand.

He hadn't had too many people ride the bull yet, and he had to admit, he was finding it a pretty damn enjoyable novelty.

The woman tossed her head, her tan cowboy hat staying in place while her blond curls went wild around her shoulders. She wrapped her hands around the harness on top of the mechanical creature and hoisted herself up. Her movements were unsteady, and he had a feeling, based on the amount of time the group had been here, and how often the men in the group had come and gone from the bar, that she was more than a little bit tipsy.

Best seat in the house. He always had the best seat in the house.

She glanced up as she situated herself and he got a good look at her face. There was a determined glint in her eyes, her brows locked together, her lips pursed into a tight circle. She wasn't just tipsy, she was pissed. Looking down at the bull like it was her own personal Everest and she was determined to conquer it along with her rage. He wondered what a bedazzled little thing like her had to be angry about. A broken nail, maybe. A pair of shoes that she really wanted that was unavailable in her size.

She nodded once, her expression growing even *more* determined as she signaled the employee Ace had operating the controls tonight.

Ace moved nearer to the bar, planting his hands flat on the surface. "This probably won't end well."

The patrons at the bar turned their heads toward the scene. And he noticed Jack's posture go rigid. "Is that—"

"Yes," Kate said.

The mechanical bull pitched forward and the petite blonde sitting on top of it pitched right along with it. She managed to stay seated, but in Ace's opinion that was a miracle. The bull went back again, and the woman straightened, arching her back and thrusting her breasts forward, her head tilted upward, the overhead lighting bathing her pretty face in a golden glow. And for a moment, just a moment, she looked like a graceful, dirty angel getting into the rhythm of the kind of riding Ace preferred above anything else.

Then the great automated beast pitched forward again and the little lady went over the top, down onto the mats underneath. There were howls from her so-called friends as they enjoyed her deposition just a little too much.

She stood on shaky legs and walked back over to the group, picking up a shot glass and tossing back another, her face twisted into an expression that suggested this was not typical behavior for her.

Kate frowned and got up from her stool, making her way over to the other woman.

Ace had a feeling he should know the woman's name, had a feeling that he probably did somewhere in the back corner of his mind. He knew everyone. Which meant that he knew a lot *about* a lot of people, recognized nearly every face he passed on the street. He could usually place them with their most defining life moments, as those were the things that often spilled out on the bar top after a few shots too many.

But it didn't mean he could put a name to every face. There were simply too many of them.

"Who is that?" he asked.

"Sierra West," Jack said, something strange in his tone.

"Oh, right."

He knew the West family well enough, or rather, he knew of them. Everyone did. Though they were hardly the type to frequent his establishment. Sierra did, which would explain why she was familiar, though they never made much in the way of conversation. She was the type who was always absorbed in her friends or her cell phone when she came to place her order. No deep confessionals from Sierra over drinks.

He'd always found it a little strange she patronized his bar when the rest of the West family didn't.

Dive bars weren't really their thing.

He imagined mechanical bulls probably weren't, either. Judging not just on Sierra's pedigree, but on the poor performance.

"No cotillions going on tonight, I guess," Ace said.

Jack turned his head sharply, his expression dark. "What's that supposed to mean?"

"Nothing."

He didn't know why, but his statement had clearly offended Monaghan. Ace wasn't in the business of voicing his opinion. He was in the business of listening. Listening and serving. No one needed to know his take on a damn thing. They just wanted a sounding board to voice their own opinions and hear them echoed back.

Typically, he had no trouble with that. This had been a little slipup.

"She's not so bad," Jack said.

Sierra was a friend of Jack's fiancée, that much was obvious. Kate was over there talking to her, expression concerned. Sierra still looked mutinous. Ace was starting to wonder if she was mad at the entire world, or if something in particular had set her off.

"I'm sure she isn't." He wasn't sure of any such thing. In fact, if he knew one thing about the world and all the people in it, it was that there was a particular type who used their every advantage in life to take whatever they wanted, whenever they wanted it, regardless of promises made. Whether they were words whispered in the dark or vows spoken in front of whole crowds of loved ones.

He was a betting man. And he would lay odds that Sierra West was one of those people. She was the type. Rich, a big fish in the small pond of the community and beautiful. That combination pretty much guaranteed her whatever she wanted. And when the option for *whatever you wanted* was available, very few people resisted it.

Hell, why would you? There were a host of things he would change if he had infinite money and power.

But just because he figured he'd be in the same boat if he were rich and almighty didn't mean he had to like it on others.

HE LOOKED BACK over at Kate, who patted her friend on the shoulder before shaking her head and walking back toward the group. "She didn't want to come sit with us or anything," Kate said, looking frustrated.

The Garrett-Monaghan crew lingered at the bar for another couple of hours before they were replaced by another set of customers. Sierra's group thinned out a little bit, but didn't disperse completely. A couple of the guys were starting to get rowdy, and Ace was starting to think he was going to have to play the part of his own bouncer tonight. It wouldn't be the first time.

Fortunately, the noisier members of the group slowly trickled outside. He watched as Sierra got up and made her way back to the bathroom, leaving a couple of girls—one of whom he assumed was the designated driver—sitting at the table.

The tab was caught up, so he didn't really care how it all went down. He wasn't a babysitter, after all.

He turned, grabbed a rag out of the bucket beneath the counter and started to wipe it down. When he looked up again, the girls who had been sitting at the table were gone, and Sierra West was standing in the center of the room looking around like she was lost.

Then she glanced his way, and her eyes lit up like a sinner looking at salvation.

Wrong guess, honey.

She wandered over to the bar, her feet unsteady. "Did you see where my friends went?"

She had that look about her. Like a lost baby deer. All wide, dewy eyes and unsteady limbs. And damned if she wasn't cute as hell.

"Out the door," he said, almost feeling sorry for her. Almost.

She wasn't the first pretty young drunk to get ditched in his bar by stupid friends. She was also exactly the kind of woman he avoided at all costs, no matter how cute or seemingly vulnerable she was.

"What?" She swayed slightly. "They weren't supposed to leave me."

She sounded mystified. Completely dumbfounded that anyone would ever leave her high and dry.

"I figured," he said. "Here's a tip—get better friends."

She frowned. "They're the best friends I have."

He snorted. "That's a sad story."

She held up her hand, the broad gesture out of place coming from such a refined creature. "Just a second."

"Sure."

She turned away, heading toward the door and out to the parking lot.

He swore. He didn't know if she had a car out there, but she was way too skunked to drive.

"Watch the place, Jenna," he said to one of the waitresses, who nodded and assumed a rather important-looking position with her hands flat on the bar and a rag in her hand, as though she were ready to wipe crumbs away with serious authority.

He rounded the counter and followed the same path Sierra had just taken out into the parking lot. He looked around for a moment and didn't see her. Then he looked down and there she was, sitting on the edge of the curb. "Everything okay?"

That was a stupid question; he already knew the answer.

She looked up. "No."

He let out a long-drawn-out sigh. The problem was, he'd followed her out here. If he had just let her walk out the door, then nothing but the pine trees and the seagulls would have been responsible for her. But no, he'd had to follow. He'd been concerned about her driving. And now he would have to follow through on that concern.

"You don't have a ride?"

She shook her head, looking miserable. "Everyone left me. Because they aren't nice. You're right. I do need better friends."

"Yes," he said, "you do. And let me go ahead and tell you right now, I won't be one of them. But as long as you don't live somewhere ridiculous like Portland, I can give you a ride home."

And this, right here, was the curse of owning a bar. Whether he should or not, he felt responsible in these situations. She was compromised, it was late, and she was alone. He could not let her meander her way back home. Not when he could easily see that she got there safely.

"A ride?" She frowned, her delicate features lit dramatically by the security light hanging on the front of the bar.

"I know your daddy probably told you not to take rides from strangers, but trust me, I'm the safest bet around. Unless you want to call someone." He checked his watch. "It's inching close to last call. I'm betting not very many people are going to come out right now."

She shook her head slowly. "Probably not."

He sighed heavily, reaching into his pocket and wrapping his fingers around his keys. "All right, come on. Get in the truck."

SIERRA LOOKED UP at her unlikely, bearded, plaid-clad savior. She knew who he was, of course. Ace Thompson was the owner of the bar, and she bought beer from him at least twice a month when she came out with her friends. They'd exchanged money and drinks across the counter more times than she could recall, but this was more words than she'd ever exchanged with him in her life.

She was angry at herself. For getting drunk. For going out with the biggest jerks in the local rodeo club. For getting on the back of a mechanical bull and opening herself up to their derision—because honestly, when you put your drunk self up on a fake, bucking animal, you pretty much deserved it. And most of all, for sitting down in the parking lot acting like she was going to cry just because she had been ditched by said jerky friends.

Oh, and being *caught* at what was most definitely an epic low made it all even worse. He'd almost certainly seen her inglorious dismount off the mechanical bull, then witnessed everyone leaving without her.

She'd been so sure today couldn't get any worse.

She'd been wrong.

"I'm fine," she said, and she could have bitten off her own tongue, because she wasn't fine. As much as she wanted to pretend she didn't need his help, she kind of did. Granted, she could call Colton or Madison. But if her sister had to drive all the way down to town from the family estate she would probably kill Sierra. And if she called Colton's house his fiancée would probably kill Sierra.

Either way, that made for a dead Sierra.

She wasn't speaking to her father. Which, really, was the root of today's evil.

"Sure you are. *Most* girls who end up sitting on their behinds at 1:00 a.m. in a parking lot are just fine."

She blinked, trying to bring his face into focus. He refused to be anything but a fuzzy blur. "I am."

For some reason, her stubbornness was on full display, and most definitely outweighed her common sense. That was probably related to the alcohol. And to the fact that all of her restraint had been torn down hours ago. Sometime early this morning when she had screamed at her father and told him she never wanted to see him again, because she'd found out he was a liar. A cheater.

Right, so that was probably why she was feeling rebellious. Angry in general. But she probably shouldn't direct it at the person who was offering a helping hand.

"Don't make me ask you twice, Sierra. It's going to make me get real grumpy, and I don't think you'll like that." Ace shifted his stance, crossing his arms over his broad chest—she was pretty sure it was broad, either that or she was seeing double—and looked down at her.

She got to her wobbly feet, pitching slightly to the side before steadying herself. Her head was spinning, her stomach churning, and she was just mad. Because she felt like crap. Because she knew better than to drink like this, at least when she wasn't in the privacy of her own home.

"Which truck?" she asked, rubbing her forehead.

He turned, not waiting for her, and began to walk across the parking lot. She followed as quickly as she could. Fortunately, the lot was mostly empty, so she didn't have to watch much but the back of Ace as they made their way to the vehicle. It wasn't a new, flashy truck. It was old, but it was in good condition. Better than most she'd seen at such an advanced age. But then, Ace wasn't a rancher. He owned a bar, so it wasn't like his truck saw all that much action.

She stood in front of the passenger-side door for a long moment before realizing he was not coming around to open it for her. Her face heated as she jerked open the door for herself and climbed up inside.

It had a bench seat. And she found herself clinging to the door, doing her best to keep the expansive seat between them as wide as possible. She was suddenly conscious of the fact that he was a very large man. Tall, broad, muscular. She'd known that, somewhere in the back of her mind. But the way he filled up the cab of a truck containing just the two of them was much more significant than the way he filled the space in a vast and crowded bar.

He started the engine, saying nothing as he put the truck in Reverse and began to pull out of the lot. She looked straight ahead, desperate to find something to say. The silence was oppressive, heavy around them. It made her feel twitchy, nervous. She always knew what to say. She was in command of every social situation she stepped into. People found her charming, and if they didn't, they never said otherwise. Because she was Sierra West, and her family name carried with it the burden of mandatory respect from the people of Copper Ridge.

She took a deep breath, trying to ease the pressure in her chest, trying to remove the weight that was sitting there.

"What's your sign?" Somehow, her fuzzy brain had retrieved that as a conversation starter. The moment the words left her mouth she wanted to stuff them back in and swallow them.

To her surprise, he laughed. “Caution.”

“What?”

“I’m a caution sign, baby. And it would be in your best interest to obey the warning…”

Don’t miss what happens when Sierra
doesn’t heed his advice in
ONE NIGHT CHARMER
by USA TODAY *bestselling author Maisey Yates!*

COMING NEXT MONTH FROM

Available May 10, 2016

#2443 TWINS FOR THE TEXAN

Billionaires and Babies • by Charlene Sands

When Brooke McKay becomes pregnant after a one-night stand with a sexy rancher, she tracks him down to discover he's a widower struggling with toddler twins! Can she help as his nanny before falling in love—and delivering her baby bombshell?

#2444 IN PURSUIT OF HIS WIFE

Texas Cattleman's Club: Lies and Lullabies

by Kristi Gold

A British billionaire and his convenient wife wed for all the wrong reasons...and she can't stay when he won't open his heart, even though their desire is undeniable. But now that she's pregnant, the stakes for their reunion are even higher...

#2445 SECRET BABY SCANDAL

Bayou Billionaires • by Joanne Rock

Wealthy football star Jean-Pierre despises the media. When rumors fly, he knows who to blame—the woman who's avoided him since their red-hot night together. His proposition: pretend they're a couple to end the scandal. But Tatiana has secrets of her own...

#2446 THE CEO'S LITTLE SURPRISE

Love and Lipstick • by Kat Cantrell

CEO Gage Branson isn't above seducing his ex, rival CEO Cassandra Clare, for business, but when he's accused of the corporate espionage threatening Cassie's company, it gets personal fast. And then he finds out someone's been hiding a little secret...

#2447 FROM FRIEND TO FAKE FIANCÉ

Mafia Moguls • by Jules Bennett

Mobster Mac O'Shea is more than willing to play fiancé with his sexy best friend at a family wedding. But it doesn't take long for Mac to realize the heat between them is all too real...

#2448 HIS SEDUCTION GAME PLAN

Sons of Privilege • by Katherine Garbera

Ferrin is the only one who can clear Hunter's name, and Hunter isn't above using charm to persuade her. He says he's only interested in the secrets she protects—so why can't he get his enemy's daughter out of his mind?

SPECIAL EXCERPT FROM

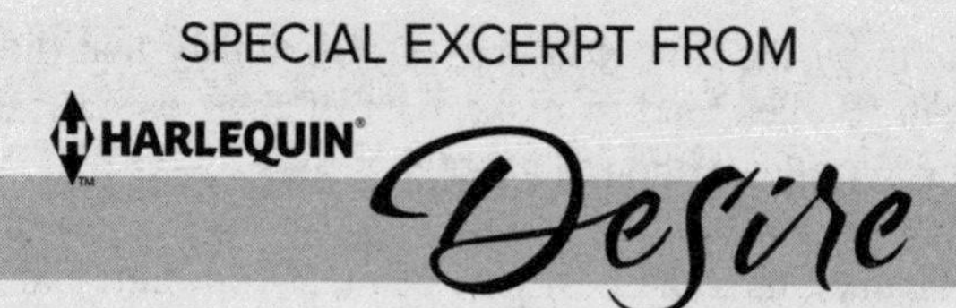

When Brooke becomes pregnant after a one-night stand with a sexy rancher, she tracks him down to discover he's a widower struggling with toddler twins! Can she help as his nanny before falling in love—and delivering her baby bombshell?

Read on for a sneak peek of
TWINS FOR THE TEXAN
the latest book by USA TODAY *bestselling author*
Charlene Sands *in the bestselling*
BILLIONAIRES AND BABIES *series*

Grateful to have made it without getting lost, Brooke had to contend with the fact she was *here*. And now, one way or another, her life was going to change forever. She rang the doorbell. A moment later, she stood face-to-face with Wyatt.

Who was holding a squirming baby boy.

It was the last thing she expected.

"Wyatt?" She was rendered speechless, staring at the man who'd made her insides quiver just one month ago.

"Come in, Brooke. I'm glad you made it."

She stared at him, still not believing what she was seeing. He'd never mentioned having a child. Although, there'd seemed to be a silent agreement between them not to delve too deeply into their private lives.

She stepped inside and Wyatt closed the door behind her. "This is Brett, my son. He was supposed to be

HDEXP0416R

sleeping by the time you arrived. Obviously that didn't happen. Babies tend to make liars of their parents, and it's been rough without a nanny."

"He's beautiful."

"Thanks, he's the best part of me. Well, him and his twin, Brianna."

"There's two of them?"

"I want to explain. Why don't you have a seat?" He started walking and she followed. "You look pretty, by the way," he said, his cowboy charm taking hold again, and she had trouble remembering how he'd dumped her after a spectacular night of sex.

A night when they'd conceived a child.

"You didn't tell me you had children."

"I just wanted to be me—not a father, not a widower—that night. My friends are forever saying I need to find myself again. That's what I was trying to do."

She inhaled a sharp breath, everything becoming clear.

If she were brave, she'd reveal her pregnancy to Wyatt and try to cope with the decisions they would make together. But her courage failed her. How could she tell this widower with twins he was about to be a father again?